LIMINAL LIVES

JENNY TOUPIN

ISBN: 979-8-9892260-2-3

Copyright © December 2024 by Jenny Toupin

All rights reserved. No part of this publication may be reproduced, stored, or transmitted in any form by any means, electronic, mechanical, photocopying, recording, scanning, or otherwise without written permission from the publisher. It is illegal to copy this book, post it to a website, or distribute it by any means without permission.

First Edition.

TABLE OF CONTENTS

CHAPTER 1

Alison and Xander cried and screamed over Evelyn's dying body, louder than the muffled sounds of the monster clawing the other side of the bathroom door. Evelyn's husband, Aaron, snarled and groaned, chewing and banging on the wood, desperate to get inside, to do things to his wife and children which would be unfathomable if there truly were a god.

Evelyn was bleeding out fast, her blood on poor Alison's hands. Xander yelled for Alison to help him stop the bleeding, but it was too late for that. Evelyn had already lost too much.

If she could laugh, Evelyn would. She had spent her entire career as a nurse helping others, only to be helpless in her own time of need.

There was nothing her children could do to save her. Evelyn wanted to scream at them to leave, tell them to save themselves. Their mother was already good as dead. Alison and Xander were wasting time. Evelyn's heart would have been riddled with anxiety, beating out of her chest, if death weren't pacing it down to an arrhythmic knock.

The wood on the door started to split.

Aaron would barge in soon and kill his children. Evelyn's children.

Evelyn saw death all the time. In the hospital, it happened at least once a month, even in their small town, but a lot more when Evelyn worked in hospice. She was numb to the concept of death.

Aaron had died—there was no mistaking it.

But.

This thing had taken over. This was not him, but yet, it was.

Aaron was a man who had loved his family more than anything. He stayed up for days when Alison had colic as a baby, volunteered to coach softball for free at Xander's elementary school, cooked dinner at least half of the time, and left notes in the kids' lunch boxes, even when they got old enough and embarrassed and told him to stop.

The creature in the hallway wasn't that man. Not anymore.

Evelyn's life flashed before her eyes, but her last moments were painfully staked to the top. The trauma of losing her husband, herself, and everything—*everyone*—within a matter of minutes was too terrible to let go of. Blood loss had made her too weak to help her children escape. As much as she wanted to be there in her children's final moments, she couldn't protect them in her condition, and Evelyn didn't want to witness what Aaron would do to them when he finally broke down that door.

The knob became loose. There wasn't much time.

Just moments ago, she had been attempting to save his life. Just moments ago, he had died.

When Aaron stopped breathing, Evelyn had gone into work mode. She recorded his time of death: 5:58 p.m., July 25, 2034.

It appeared he had suffered a cardiac arrest, but he ran two miles every day before work, had no pre-existing conditions, got screened for everything you could think of, and in fact, was a complete hypochondriac and always had been.

That was how he and Evelyn had met. She was a young receptionist, and she had thought Aaron kept coming into the doctor's office to see her. That wasn't the case initially, but eventually, it was.

For a while, Evelyn had assumed he only married her for her medical insight. Aaron would joke she was right, then ask her if the mole on his back might be cancer.

Evelyn never laughed at his jokes, but that didn't stop him from making them.

His eyes had gone murky, so she shut them.

***

(One hour earlier)

"Amen," Evelyn whispered.

The family had been at the dinner table when Aaron started clearing his throat and acting strange. Evelyn spoke over his struggles, leading evening prayer.

"Bless us, O Lord, and these thy gifts."

The children joined in. Alison had spoken every word deliberately, while Xander mumbled. Evelyn gave Aaron a look, but Aaron couldn't catch his breath.

"From thy bounty…"

Aaron coughed and furrowed his brows, hacking out something wet. He grabbed his chest with one hand, his fork erect in the other, and looked at Evelyn to save him, an expression of silent panic on his face.

In synchrony, Evelyn and the children rose from their seats.

Evelyn recognized it quickly and ran to his aid, instructing Alison to call 911. She asked Xander to come help her.

But then something strange happened. Aaron convulsed, like he was having a seizure, and violently slumped over onto the table. His fork went right through his cheek. Blood spurted in small squirts. That's when it became chaos.

Evelyn managed to get Aaron to the floor and attempted chest compressions. Full-on CPR would have been dangerous and wouldn't have worked, considering the wound.

"Mom! Mom!" Alison came rushing back in a fret. "I tried your phone. Dad's phone. They're not working!"

Evelyn knew 911 would never make it in time. And that's when Aaron's last breath abandoned him. That's when Aaron left his wife and two children behind. And the thing they truly needed saving from was growing inside of his fresh corpse.

"Dad! Dad! Mom! Do something! Is Dad dead? Mom!" Xander screamed at Evelyn.

"Run to the Pilson's place," Evelyn instructed Alison.

She was the faster runner. Alison was on the track team at school.

"Use their phone to call 911, then come straight back here."

Alison nodded and was through the door in an instant.

Evelyn ushered Xander from the dining area to the living room, out of sight of Aaron's body. Poor Xander was hyperventilating and calling for his daddy like a little boy. He was fourteen, which wasn't so little anymore, but in that moment, he was allowed to be. Alison was older but usually more immature. She was ready to start her senior year in the fall, after the quietus of summer. It wasn't supposed to be like this.

Xander perked up and his eyes dried when gunshots resonated from outside. Alison wasn't back yet. Evelyn had to save her.

"Stay here!" she yelled at Xander, who was already running to his room.

Evelyn whipped open the front door, and Alison barreled into her arms. She went to embrace her shaken child, but Alison was pushing her out of the way, yelling at Evelyn to move.

"Go! We have to go!" Alison shouted.

She shoved her mother back into the house and slammed the front door. Alison put her back up against it and slid down, her hands against her temples.

Evelyn was ready to strike. She knelt level with her daughter and wiped the tear-soaked strands of hair from her face.

"What happened, Alison? Talk to me!"

"M-M-Mr. P-Pilson. He-He was. Ea-Ea-Ea…" Alison stuttered.

She was trembling and her teeth chattered. Her cheeks were blotched red, similar to the veins popping in her puffy, watery eyes. Like she were a baby again, Evelyn pulled Alison to her chest and let her cry. She patted her daughter's back and shushed her, signaling it was fine, that she was okay now.

Evelyn dismissed her daughter's behavior. Alison had just witnessed the sudden, violent death of her father. The Pilson's probably weren't home. Gunshots pervaded outside, but Evelyn swallowed her concern to focus on her kids—her home.

She's in shock. That's that.

Evelyn had no way of knowing what was going on out there, but sirens grew closer. A small notion flourished inside her mind, signaling the Pilson's were in trouble, but it was washed away by her own tragedy.

Evelyn finally realized something was off when there was a giant *thump* at the door behind her daughter. Alison screamed and crawled away from her mother's grasp, shouting for her brother. Evelyn rose to her feet. There were three more loud strikes followed by rapid gunfire. Instinctively, Evelyn crouched, but her curiosity led her to the window.

Mr. Pilson's corpse was on the porch, with fresh bullet wounds in his head—a fragment of the neighbor he once was.

Evelyn couldn't stand the sight of any more blood. She had a strong stomach, but vomit curled up her esophagus and came firing out.

A giant gash of dried blood, puss, and black gunk protruded from Mr. Pilson's shoulder blade. Shards of bone were sprinkled in places they shouldn't have been.

Mr. Pilson's shoulder was gruesome, and the injury wasn't fresh. He surely would have died from blood loss with a wound that size. But he was on her porch, bullets in his brain, and no fresh blood was soaking into the concrete.

Evelyn peeked through her shear curtains. No. He hadn't died from those gunshot wounds.

But how?

Loud explosions in the near distance shook the house. Vases, picture frames, and school art projects fell to the floor and broke. More gunshots echoed in the neighborhood.

Scampering footsteps rushed into the living room, where Evelyn spied on the outside.

"Mom! Look at the news. Turn on the TV!" Xander said.

He became impatient and ended up turning on the TV himself. A national broadcast alarm blared through the room. The emergency alert was on repeat. Stay indoors. Remain calm. An immediate curfew was in place until further notice.

"Come here," Evelyn said. She herded her children into her arms. "It will be okay."

She didn't believe the words of assurance she gave her children. But she clung onto the hope they did, and that was good enough.

Another explosion landed nearby. This one was loud and stronger than the last.

After the crashing of more things hitting the floor from shelves and tables, the house became oddly silent. The kids quieted their sobs and perked up their ears. Alison's eyes widened, and she squeezed her mother tightly.

"What is it?" Evelyn asked.

"Did you hear that noise? In the kitchen?"

A clash of pots and pans startled the family.

Their eyes strayed from the television, and they stood, like deer in headlights. Evelyn turned toward the kitchen doorway, not knowing what was around the corner.

The shuffling of another person, socks dragging against the vinyl floor. The groan…

The guttural noise dragged out like an ominous growl, a signal to keep away. To run. But Evelyn, Alison, and Xander couldn't move, struck immobile by fear.

The shuffling and moaning grew louder, drawing closer to the doorway. Silverware clanked to the linoleum floor, along with other larger items that couldn't be discerned. Evelyn's heart pounded in her chest, and she instinctively moved to shield her children.

Her eyes shifted to the left, to the dining room, where only a bloody imprint was left of Aaron's body. Speckles of crimson painted the ground toward the kitchen.

The creature stumbled into view, its once-familiar face twisted into a grotesque mask of death. Whatever was coming out of the kitchen was not human—at least, not anymore.

It was Aaron.

Or rather, what was left of him.

His eyes were glazed over, empty, and he lurched toward them, arms outstretched, fingers curled into claws. A surge of conflicting emotions seized Evelyn—horror, grief, and a strange sense of detachment. Nothing mattered but protecting her children. No matter how much she ached for her husband to be alive, to be the one fighting for them, he wasn't. Aaron was gone.

Her children yelled, backing themselves into a corner.

Evelyn grabbed the closest thing to her—a nearby lamp. She yanked it, cord and all, from the outlet and swung it at Aaron's head.

The lamp shattered on impact, but Aaron kept coming, unfazed. Evelyn grabbed the entire end table and lunged at Aaron, pushing him to the other side of the room. He fell by the front door. She took this moment to rush her children toward the hall, in the direction of the bedrooms, where she planned to climb out a window with them.

That's when he got her.

Aaron yanked Evelyn's hand from behind and pulled her with primal strength. He sunk his teeth into her skin, ripping apart her flesh like a dog with a new toy. Aaron gnawed through the muscle, the tissue, all the way to the bone. Strands of tendons tore when Evelyn jerked her arm from her husband's grip. Pieces of her hung from his mouth. He clacked his teeth together, and remnants of her body slumped from his jaws and onto the carpet.

Blood gushed from Evelyn's wound. She fell on her bottom and scooted away with her feet, shaking violently, in shock from the gash on her arm. Aaron moved deliberately now, inspecting the shredded meat and blood on his hands. He seemed to be savoring her taste. Aaron got down on the ground, like he was about to leap at his family, but instead, he trailed at a steady pace, gobbling up the blood trail from the carpet.

He grunted and groaned, the fibers stuck between his teeth. Evelyn shook and cried, holding her arm and wincing in pain.

It all happened so fast then.

Alison grabbed her mother from under her arms and dragged her into the closest room—the bathroom. Aaron made a clicking noise and contorted his neck, flaring his nostrils.

He charged.

A barrage of bullets hit him in the chest, stunning him and knocking him back.

Xander stood trembling in the hall next to the bathroom. His sister yelled at him to come in and close the door, but he remained frozen for a moment. Aaron didn't go down. Xander unloaded the rest of the gun into his father, striking him in the chest and the stomach and grazing his cheek. Fourteen bullets later and his father still persisted.

He had shot his dad with his own gun. A Glock 19, which Aaron kept in the drawer of his nightstand.

The echoing of the rapid fire in the enclosed space was deafening. Aaron hadn't been a firearm connoisseur, but a strong believer in his Second Amendment rights. He was always trying to take his son to the shooting range, but Xander had never been interested, preferring to stay in and use guns in video games.

Evelyn was in and out of consciousness. But she did hear the bathroom door slam and both of her children frantically shouting and arguing. She tried to sit up using the toilet bowl as leverage, but her hands were coated in blood and slick. Evelyn slipped and hurt herself further. She was on the brink of passing out, but she was determined. Evelyn couldn't leave her kids.

But she was dying.

Sweat leaked from her pores as fast as the blood was coming out. Her insides burned. A feverish Evelyn suddenly felt ravenous and feral. It hurt so bad, she wanted to rip her skin off. She scratched at her open wound.

Alison broke out of the fight with her brother. "Mom, stop! You have to stop the bleeding." She took off her hoodie and wrapped it around Evelyn's arm.

Aaron was at the door, throwing himself against it and making awful, monstrous sounds.

"Phones are still not working!" Xander said. "I don't know what to do. Fuck." He dropped the Glock to the ground. It slid in the river of blood leading from Evelyn. With no bullets left, it was useless now, not that shooting Aaron had done anything but slow him down.

"Language," Evelyn muttered.

Tears welled in her son's eyes. "Mom. Everything will be okay. Won't it, Alison? Tell Mom she'll be okay."

Aaron was at the bottom of the door, licking the blood trail. His chalky tongue curled, getting whatever scraps he could.

Alison whined and Xander hopped back, pacing in the small area.

Aaron relentlessly pounded at the door. The kids huddled around Evelyn with towels and clothes that had been tussled along the bathroom floor, attempting to stop the blood. But it kept coming. Evelyn's face became gray and her breathing labored. Her chest rattled, each inhalation a battle.

"Stop the bleeding!" yelled Xander.

"I'm trying! I'm trying!"

But it was too late.

Evelyn tried to part her lips to tell her kids to stop fighting. To give them one last reassurance everything was going to be okay.

The taste of copper and salt numbed her tongue. Her entire body tingled, and her vision became static. Then darkness. Her body rotted in real time, the sickly sweet aroma wafting up into her nostrils. She took one last breath out.

Her children's screaming grew fainter.

Evelyn desperately wanted to demand for her children to back away. Climb through the window above the tub. Escape. She was becoming whatever this sickness was that her husband had. And if he didn't kill her children, she feared she would.

Alison and Xander watched in horror while their mother's eyes glazed over. Xander shook Evelyn and pleaded for her to wake up. Alison took charge then, grabbing her brother by the forearm.

"Xander, we have to go," she said.

"We can't leave her here! Dad will kill her."

He jerked his arm away and rushed back to his mother's side. Xander took her limp palm and cupped his own cheek with it, crying into his mother's hand.

"I love you, Mom," he said.

Alison couldn't even look at her. She bit her lip and glanced away, tears building up in her eyes.

"Come on," she urged. "Let's go."

Aaron banged louder on the door. The hinges slowly started to pop. The top one broke off, and he put his dead weight on the wood to topple it over.

The kids screamed and shoved each other, trying to get to the window first. Alison made it out and reached her hand back to help Xander. He was short and in need of a growth spurt.

Xander wheezed, easily winded, trying to hoist himself up to the window. "I can't breathe," he said.

"Fucking try!"

The wood of the door finally snapped, and Aaron came barreling through. He snarled and staggered to his feet.

In a burst of adrenaline, Alison grabbed onto her brother and pulled hard, like her arms were rope. Xander caught his bearings and was nearly out of the window when his father grabbed his foot.

The kids screamed, and at the last minute, when Dad was about to chomp down, Xander kicked him square in the face, causing Aaron to tumble backward onto the recent corpse of their mother. With a loud thud and squish, Aaron sank into her body.

They had made it out alive. There was hope.

Evelyn had expected great nothingness after death. A prominent emptiness. But she had something still alive in her, like her blood had been replaced with liquid fire. Her nervous system had gone haywire, rapidly sending electric shocks to her brain until it fried. She grew bloated, and her head hung heavy.

Then she became hungry.

Evelyn's body convulsed with the onset of the transformation, and her consciousness slipped into a state of primal need. Her senses returned and sharpened, honing in on the scent of her children lingering in the air. Evelyn's urge to save them metamorphosed into something sinister. She found strength like she never had before. It wasn't human.

She heaved her husband off. He took one sniff but had no more interest in her, no more feral urgency. Aaron just pushed himself to his feet and hobbled out of the bathroom through the broken door.

Evelyn staggered upright, her movements jerky and uncoordinated. She opened her mouth to speak, to yell the names of her children, but words wouldn't come out—only a horrifying moan. Aaron grunted back from the next room. Evelyn's legs were solid, like tree trunks. She intended to move them, to lunge forward, but they wouldn't obey.

The pain inside became unbearable, more than her final moments of life. Her jaws clacked together, grinding her teeth. Her right arm slumped to her side, barely hanging on by strands of remaining muscle. But it hurt no more than the rest of her body. There were only two senses she felt over all else: agony and hunger.

Thoughts of concern and worry for her children loitered in the dark chasms of her mind. Her frontal lobe pulsed in the worst headache she had ever had. Thanks to nursing school, Evelyn knew all the functions of the brain. The frontal lobe was what controlled impulses in humans, as well as motor functions.

If Evelyn had been alive and examining a patient, she would work through this logically. But presumably, all her other components of her brain should have been dead. Though, that wasn't the case at all. Not dead, just not at full power.

Her olfactory bulb flared, and she pounced at the ground in the pool of her own blood. Her nostrils flared when she sniffed it. The smell was pleasing, but there were plenty of scents around Evelyn making her cringe: the stale toilet water, the debris of feces on the toilet scrubber brush, and even the mildew nestling in the air vents.

Her temporal lobe throbbed, like turning on a light switch. The sounds of chaos outside her suburban bungalow returned. But rather than them being overwhelming and crashing into each other in a cacophony of discord, each held its own note.

Last to come back was her sight.

This sense was dull in comparison to the rest. It was grainy, like looking through a television that still used an antenna. Evelyn tried to tune her signal and focus. But when she did so, her frontal lobe thrummed harder, and the pain became too immense. Speckles of magenta and lime green filtered over her otherwise monochrome vision.

CHAPTER 2

Xander and Alison didn't stop to catch their breath. They ran past the dilapidated play structure of their youth, through Evelyn's vegetable garden, and straight toward the fence. Just like they did when they were younger, they lodged their feet into the holes of the chain link and hoisted themselves over into their neighbor Sal's yard.

Sal was younger than Alison but older than Xander. He had fawned after Alison since he was five, but she had no interest. Sal at first had no desire to play with Xander, but as they got older and Alison didn't want to hang out with boys anymore, Sal and Xander had become tight friends.

The two families had always been close. It wasn't unusual for Sal to just walk in their door on a Wednesday afternoon and raid the snack cupboard. The same went for Alison and Xander. Sal's family was a second home for them, and it was a no-brainer to go to them for help.

After both kids hopped the fence into Sal's yard, they scampered to the sliding glass door. It had always been unlocked, but today it wasn't.

"Sal! Sal! Open up. Please, man, open up," Xander begged.

"Sal, please, we need you!"

They both thrashed on the glass until Sal came into view.

There was a glimmer of insanity in his eyes when he rounded the corner into his dining room. His pupils were large, and his face and clothes were soiled in blood. In his right hand, he gripped a baseball bat also tainted with red. He observed them through the glass from a distance.

Xander and Alison continued to pound on the door. Screams and dust from the barrage of nearby gunfire surrounded them.

Sal hesitated, his grip tightening on the bloodied bat, his mind most likely a chaotic whirlpool of his own horrors. But then he seemed to register the genuine terror in Alison's eyes, the same girl he had admired for years, and something inside him appeared to snap back to reality.

"Alison," Sal whispered.

He dropped the bat and ran to the door to unlock it, but he froze for a moment, looking at them. His finger leveraged on the lock, Sal bit his lip.

"Are you two sick?" he asked. "Did their blood get on you?

"No, Sal. Please, man. Our mom is dead. Our dad…You have to let us in. Please!" Xander shouted.

"Before they get us, please, Sal, please," Alison said quietly. She kept repeating, "Please," banging her head against the glass.

Xander and Alison practically tumbled over when Sal finally opened the door.

"Move! Quick! Get in before I change my mind," said Sal.

Xander and Alison scrambled inside, and Sal swiftly slid the door shut, locking it behind them. But their relief was temporary as they took in the condition of the house. It was ransacked, with broken furniture and signs of struggle everywhere. The other people in Sal's household were nowhere to be seen.

Neither Xander nor Alison asked where they were due to a sinking suspicion Sal had undergone a similar battle to the one they just had. Sal had a large family: his father, mother, abuela, his older brothers Miguel and Eddy, and his younger sister, Gabby.

Their house had always been loud and chaotic, but today, it was eerie. The chaos was all outside, and the inside of the house contained an eldritch silence.

"Well, come in," Sal said. He motioned for his friends to follow him. Around the kitchen was their living room.

Sal seemed in a trance, trudging through the massacre of his family. He stepped over the dead body of his mother, a kitchen knife sticking from the back of her head, before making his way to the couch.

Abuela sat in her wheelchair, facing the television still playing the emergency broadcast. Her features had been sunken in, no doubt by the baseball bat Sal had greeted Xander and Alison with. A mess of blood, fragments of skull, and brain gyrus sprouted from Abuela's scalp. The tea on the coffee table in front of her was still steaming.

Alison put her hand over her mouth, swallowing the vomit creeping up her throat. The stream of tears down her face hadn't stopped since it all began.

Xander jumped back and put his fists up, waiting for the corpses to reanimate. His eyes were wild, shaking within their sockets.

"Remember when we were kids, Xander?" Sal asked.

"We *are* kids." Xander's asthma was bothering him again. He choked on air and a few tears.

"We made fake blood in the garage in one of Papa's five-gallon buckets, mixing together all those strange chemicals and fluids that probably shouldn't have went together?" Sal laughed. "Papa just let us do it, though. 'Kids will be kids,' he always said."

Sal's face went soft, and he stared off into the nothingness in front of him, combing his hair through his fingertips, lost in a memory.

"We'd rip up his old shop shirts. The oil stains, grit, and dirt helped our cause," Sal continued.

"I think we should leave," Xander whispered to his sister.

"Don't go!" Sal stood up and put his hands out to his friends. "I just made a pot of tea. It's still warm. Stay and have some, won't you?"

Sal shrugged, touching back into reality for a moment. A meager pool of tears formed in his eyes. He wiped them away and streaked the blood from his arm all over his face, like war paint.

Alison ignored Xander. "Why did you ask if we had blood on us?"

"Do you?" Sal eyed Alison up and down when she approached, withdrawing in response. "Don't come any closer."

"Alison!" Xander said. "We need to move. It's not safe here."

Sal wavered, seemingly wary of his friends and perhaps wanting them to leave but also hoping to protect them at all costs. He grabbed Alison by the arm.

"Stay. Please. I need help," said Sal.

"Let her go." Xander yanked his sister back behind him. Excess blood from Sal streaked on Alison's skin.

"Why? Are you sick?" Alison asked.

She wiped the blood on a throw blanket hanging over the couch. Cheeks, Sal's gray tabby, hopped on top, teetering between it and the windowsill. It weaved through the broken blinds, purring and rubbing his puffy face on the glass, before pouncing at Alison while she wiped her hands.

Sal's eyes flickered with guilt, inspecting the blood on his own and coming to the realization his entire family was dead.

"No…I'm not sick…I have no open wounds."

Cheeks stuck his head underneath Alison's hand, which provided a moment of relief from the anxiety of Abuela's sunken face and the body at her feet. He was a pudgy, middle-aged cat. Not fat, just had the standard droopy pouch older cats tended to get. Cheeks grabbed Alison's hand and rolled on his back, kicking her with his hind feet.

"What do you think this is?" Xander asked.

He unraveled a wad of paper towel from the holder on the kitchen counter and dampened it with water from the faucet. Xander had intended to give it to Sal to wipe up his face but saw his own reflection in the kitchen window. He was mortified. His mother's blood had splattered onto his neck and stained his shirt.

Xander reluctantly touched the speckles of his mother's remains. He swallowed hard and shook his head, trying to rid himself of panic.

Sal had his arms crossed and his mind lost somewhere, either looking at Alison or through her, when Xander handed him the paper towel.

"You don't see what this is?" Sal blotted his face, sparing glances at Xander like he were an idiot.

Alison picked up Cheeks and cradled him, rocking and petting him. She booped his nose and kissed the top of his head, whispering words of affirmation in his ears. He closed his eyes in contentedness and continued to purr.

Xander folded his arms.

"Can we…talk somewhere else?" He fidgeted and pointed over at Sal's mother and Abuela, biting his lip. "I can't…be around this any longer."

"Right…" said Sal.

"Your room?"

Sal looked toward the stairs and hesitated before shaking his head.

"No. Not there. Come to the basement."

Xander nodded. "Alison, come on. Let's talk somewhere else."

But she didn't appear to hear her brother, having tuned out the outside world.

Cheeks stirred, signaling he was ready to be put down, but Alison didn't take notice. His hind legs ended up scratching Alison when he jumped into Abuela's lap.

"Ow!" yelled Alison.

The cat purred even louder while Alison inspected her wounds. It sniffed around Abuela's corpse and put his front paws on her shoulder. Cheeks investigated the body, his purrs drumming at a quicker pace.

Sal looked away. "Let's go."

He went toward the basement.

"No, Cheeks!" yelled Xander. He went to shoo the cat when it licked and nibbled at the flesh where Abuela's face used to be. "Scram."

"Little bastard got me good," Alison said.

She was oblivious to everything around her. Xander pleaded for Alison to come with him after Sal, and she finally blindly followed.

Sal led the way down to the basement, his footsteps echoing in the narrow stairwell. The musty smell of dampness permeated the air. Sal's house was old, and the basement had probably never been cleaned. Cobwebs lined the open stairs, and pieces of the railing were broken and missing. Gray paint chips had been picked at and painted, time and time again, over the dirt.

A single overhead bulb cast a muted yellow light over the cluttered space. Boxes of old clothes and holiday decorations had been stacked haphazardly against the walls.

A vintage life-size Santa was posed in a wave, greeting them at the bottom of the stairwell. It had always creeped them out when they were kids. They would play hide and scare all the time, and as a prank, someone would always move the Santa around in unexpected places. For once, that Santa wasn't on the kids' minds.

Sal pulled up a crate, emptied the junk out, and sat on top of it. A cloud of dust rose when Alison plopped down on an old smoke-stained couch, still clutching her scratched arm, eyes distant. Xander paced back and forth, his mind racing.

"We need a plan," he said. "We can't just sit here and wait for things to get worse."

"It's the zombie apocalypse, brother. We've been training our whole lives for this," Sal said. "Grab some weapons and we bash heads in. There ain't no way around it."

"This isn't a fucking video game." Xander got up in Sal's face, spit spraying his friend as he shouted. "My dad is dead. My mom is dead. Your entire fucking family: dead. Get serious, Sal. God."

Alison finally spoke out. "Don't talk to him like that, Xander. You're not helping."

"What do you think we should do?" asked Sal.

"First, you have to tell us what happened. You know our parents are dead. And we saw…your grandma and mom. But what about the rest of the family? Your dad, brothers, sister? Where are they?"

"Good point," said Xander.

"Dad is at work. I couldn't get ahold of him. My phone has been acting weird. Can't get a signal."

"Ours too," replied Alison. "We don't have the same service either. So it can't be that…"

"What about the others?" Xander asked.

The color on Sal's face washed away, leaving a sickly blank canvas.

"The twins were shooting hoops up at the park. Gabby…She…She, uh…"

A series of bangs upstairs interrupted Sal. He went quiet and stood up from his crate, eyes peeled on the doorway upstairs.

"Sal, what aren't you telling us?" Alison shook him.

They all flinched when another loud bang was followed by a crash. Footsteps fluttered upstairs, pacing in circles with no rhyme or reason. Whoever was up there was tearing up the house.

Sal ran to the edge of the stairwell and put his back to it, arms out, guarding the exit.

"Don't hurt her," Sal pleaded. "You can't hurt Gabby."

CHAPTER 3

Slow and steady, Evelyn's limbs started to move. It began with a twitch in her kneecap. A tingling in her calves propelled her forward. The agonizing throbs in her head made it impossible to concentrate—memories fried like eggs in a skillet at Sunday breakfast. Pain and hunger consumed her.

A pecking thought food would provide respite from the pain echoed in her head between the pulsing aches. Instinctively, Evelyn shuffled toward the kitchen and opened the fridge. The stench of leftover pizza, baked chicken, and mashed potatoes was repulsive. She groaned, standing in the pale light of the fridge while it hummed.

In desperation, she reached for the pizza box to try anyway, but her head thrummed again, and she dropped it on the floor. The box opened, and the triangle pieces slid out. Evelyn was famished, so she took what was right in front of her. She dropped to her knees and devoured the slices, engorging her cheeks with the cold sauce and hardened cheese and bread.

Immediately, Evelyn vomited the whole of what she had eaten, along with a slush of blood. She heaved over the messy pile, clenching her gut. Then she puked again—rapids of crimson mixed with a vile-smelling black and brown sludge.

Aaron stood over her, groaning. Evelyn wondered if he was sentient, like her. She grabbed onto his pants to signal for his help since she couldn't speak. He just seemed annoyed, pulling to try and get away.

His vacant eyes and sluggish movements were a stark contrast to the man she had once known. But it didn't hurt seeing him this way. There was only physical pain. Evelyn had no pity or sorrow over the death of her husband anymore, if it really was death cursing them.

The agony in her gut subsided slightly, allowing Evelyn a moment of clarity. She looked around the kitchen, her eyes darting from the fridge to the counters, searching for something, *anything*, that might help. The hunger gnawed at her insides, a relentless force driving her to find sustenance.

Then Aaron went ballistic. He rushed to the window, growling and hissing, banging his fists on the glass.

A mother and daughter, looking for somewhere to flee, screamed and stumbled away as quickly as they had run up to the house.

Like a dog barking at the mailman, Aaron was inexorable.

In defeat, Evelyn closed the fridge. She went to sigh, but instead, only a raspy groan came out.

Pinned to the fridge was a family photo they had taken the summer prior at Niagara Falls.

The kids.

That's right. She had almost forgotten about them through the fog of death. Her synapses burned in the area holding her memories of her old life. Evelyn had been so excited for the trip, even though Aaron had wished they could have left the kids at home and went as a couple. In the photo, they were on a boat. A cloud of mist was behind them, pressing up against their backs. They were all squirmed close together with a mixture of fear and smiles.

Xander had been terrified of going overboard on the Maid of the Mist, which got up close and personal with the famous waterfall. He was never the best swimmer, despite Evelyn giving both the kids swim lessons from a young age.

Despite the struggle to send the signals from her brain to her extremities, Evelyn deliberately clutched the photo between her fingertips and turned back to Aaron, who was still ferociously trying to get outside. Whatever she was, whatever he was, Evelyn decided they weren't the same.

With slow, deliberate steps, she moved away from the kitchen, her body protesting with every motion. Her mind was a storm of fragmented thoughts, but one goal remained clear: find her children. Evelyn stumbled through the hallway, the memories of happier times flickering in and out of her consciousness. The family portraits on the walls seemed to mock her with their normalcy, each smiling face a reminder of what she had lost.

Evelyn passed by Xander's room. The stench of Doritos dust and flat Mountain Dew burned her nostrils. He had been streaming on Twitch before dinner. A cartooned version of Xander held a thumbs-up with subtext that said: "We'll be right back!"

Alison's room was clean and organized. A rainbow of pastel colors lined her shelves, with organizational bins and a showcase for her track awards. Squishmallows were toppled on her bed like a mountain, leading up to her pale purple pillows. It smelled like candied peaches in her room. A stick of incense burned. The last log of soot hit the tray, and the orange light extinguished. The remainder of the smoke rose and dispersed into the air.

At the end of the hall was her and Aaron's room. The hallway seemed to stretch endlessly while she lurched toward the door. She reached for it, but another pulsing pain struck Evelyn's head.

The facade of memories burst, replaced by her returning hunger. With a guttural growl, she clutched her temples and roared out in pain. In panic, Evelyn ran away from the bedroom she had spent so many nights rotting away in, watching reality TV with her snoring husband, her only solace being her alarm blaring in her ears to signal a new day.

Evelyn pummeled toward the front entryway, sparing her husband a final glance before leaving him and her life behind. Dried blood streamed along his knuckles from pounding at the window. Small fractures had formed in the glass from his efforts.

A gust of wind smacked Evelyn in the face upon her opening the door. But instead of breathing in the fresh air, she simply allowed it to brush past her. Cicadas wailed in the treetops. The sirens of ambulances and law enforcement waned. Screams of people lessened—those who made noise were easy targets. And at Evelyn's feet was Mr. Pilson's corpse. The sight which had disturbed her earlier didn't faze her in the slightest now.

Others who looked like Evelyn paced down the street. Bodies of her friends and neighbors lined the lawns and sidewalks. Without care, Evelyn stormed through Mr. Pilson's blood bag. Her feet shuffled him aside, like kicking trash. Like his body were a cluster of maple seeds and dirt cluttering her porch.

Those seeds spun down in the front yard when the wind pressed forward. Cotton from the Pilson's dogwood tree whirled around the seedlings, like fluff fallen from the clouds. The tree scraps formed a petite tornado sweeping across the road, the crashed cars, and the corpses, both dead and undead. Except one.

An older Nissan Altima rolled up, coming to a halt when one of the zombies ran in front of the vehicle.

Evelyn's mouth watered. The smell of the rust eating away between the wheel bearings strengthened the scent of iron surrounding the woman in the driver's seat. The squeal of the brakes and sound of the impact made the other undead perk up and run toward the clatter.

Evelyn didn't recognize the woman, but it didn't matter. She was hungry, and despite a small pea-sized segment of her brain warning her against it, Evelyn wanted to taste that woman. It was erotic, just thinking about the woman's flesh between her teeth. Evelyn imagined it like a perfectly cooked braised rib, the meat slipping off the bone.

Fourteen undead surrounded the Nissan now—the numbers growing by the second—banging on the windows and desperately trying to claw their way into the vehicle. The woman cried and frantically tried to get away, but there were too many of them. The car wouldn't move. It shook and nearly flipped over from the enormous effort by the undead army.

With Evelyn eager to join, that made fifteen. She was the last bit of strength needed to break open the driver side window and scoop out the woman by her hair. The woman's begging for her life fell upon deaf ears in the struggle.

Evelyn fought for meat against the others scrambling for scraps. She elbowed them and tried her best to hoard as much of the flesh for herself as she could. The first bite was unlike anything she had ever tasted. The soft tissues melted in her mouth like a luscious cut of prime meat served with a butter-infused au jou.

The woman's screams broke off into gurgles, and blood sprouted from her throat like a burst pipe.

Evelyn's intense migraine shriveled into nothingness the more she binged. In its place, a prickling feeling in the pit of her stomach sang with joy. The exoticism of the feast made her feel more alive than she ever had in her mortal life. Groans of the horde faded off into slurping and chewing while they satiated their appetites. When Evelyn's teeth ground against the mandible of the stranger she was eating, she took reprieve.

A switch turned on in the back of her head. Her humanity shined a small light at the end of a dark tunnel. It flickered, and fresh blood dripped from her mouth. Another from the horde took Evelyn's space, chomping on the remaining bits of meat. Evelyn wiped her face and took a look around her.

Waves of undead swarmed the one body, which was mostly bone by now. Pieces of the woman had been torn from limbs and gnawed on like fried chicken.

The flickering light in the back of Evelyn's mind had different plans. Memories of her children's smiles flashed in the warmth of hope. She pictured Xander and Alison, their faces lit by the glow of birthday candles, their laughter filling the room during Christmas mornings. These memories were a stark contrast to the brutality of the moment, a reminder of the humanity she was desperately clinging to.

Evelyn moved aimlessly down the street, farther from the place she had once called home, and she let these images play out like a movie in her head.

With no concept of time, she could have been pacing for minutes or hours. It didn't matter anymore. But the day hadn't yet passed. The summer sun was dissolving over the horizon. Night would soon fall upon the once quiet town, but slumber would not.

Evelyn had no feelings of energy or lethargy. She simply existed in a plane overlapping the one that was familiar. Traveling like a chill through a desert, she carried on wherever instinct lead. Her grainy vision improved after nightfall, clearer in the darkness than it ever had been during the day.

A familiar smell froze Evelyn in place.

Succulent peaches consumed the air. It was so refreshing compared to everything else around her. The fires, corpses, and decay all paled in comparison to the fond memory.

Evelyn's fingers twitched, but she still couldn't command her muscles to move as her brain wished. She wanted to lift her head and see Alison's face. Run to her daughter and embrace her. Hold her.

Tear her limb from limb and devour her.

But behind the scent of peaches was a cool metallic aroma Evelyn could taste. Oils used to polish the metal had an acrid odor.

The sound of a pistol being reloaded came from behind Evelyn, and she understood.

CHAPTER 4

Alison's heart sank when she realized the gravity of Sal's words.

"Oh, Sal…" She proceeded with caution toward him.

"Back away," he said. "She doesn't have to die."

"If she's one of those things, she's already gone, brother," Xander replied. "You have to move so we can get out of here. There's no sense in us dying too."

"I hate to admit my brother being right at anything, but—"

"No! Fuck off. You can leave if you promise not to hurt her. I'll make sure she doesn't bother you," Sal insisted.

"Fine. Have it your way." Xander held his head. "Fuck, do I have a headache."

He rummaged through boxes and around obscure pieces of art and furniture, attempting to find something that could pass for a weapon. Light bulbs shattered on the gray-speckled floor. Sal's old Guitar Hero set crashed into the canvas of a painting Eddy had done in art class in the seventh grade. This transformed Sal's fear into a festering anger.

"Enough!" Sal said. He tackled his friend the moment Xander found a dull katana from a decorative wall set.

Xander dropped the sword, and it slid across the floor during the scuffle, landing at Alison's feet. She knew best not to interfere with the boys while they fought. They were oblivious to her words when they got this way.

Sal and Xander didn't even notice all their clamor had led Gabby right to them. She stood in the doorway, hunched over and arms out in a hook, ready to attack.

Gabby had always admired her long hair. Her mother would fix it every night in one long braid after her bath. It went down to her waist. During summer, Gabby wore nothing but a swimsuit, always in the pool from dawn until dusk. Now, her hair was still wet from the pool earlier in the day. A familiar pattern of baby sharks covered her one-piece suit.

Alison's heart pained at the thought of what she had to do next. When she reached down to grab the katana, Gabby hissed and lunged down the stairs. Alison made eye contact with the thing, trying to remind herself this wasn't her friend anymore.

Its eyes were different. Cold. Pale. Dead. Gabby was dead. Her skin was gray, and she had a huge adult-sized bite on her calf.

There was no time for empathy. This thing wasn't human. And the boys were hitting each other and shouting. Alison widened her stance, gripping the katana until her palms ached from lack of circulation. Since the blade was undoubtedly dull, Alison drew back the sword.

When Gabby was a hair away, Alison plunged the sword up the little girl's throat. It pressed into the flesh like a kabob, but the sword didn't go all the way through. Gabby wound her arms around, intending to propel forward and take a bite out of Alison.

With more force this time, with Sal and Xander finally bearing witness to what was going on, Alison performed the finishing move. She thrust the sword with impetus, up through Gabby's throat, puncturing the brain and exiting the back of her skull.

Gabby's jaw dropped, and she immediately went limp.

The little girl's lifeless body crumpled to the floor, but the katana was still lodged in her head. Alison stood over her, breathing heavily, hands trembling. She released her grip on the sword. Gabby tipped back, like a broken bottle in a carnival game.

Sal and Xander were frozen, their fight forgotten. They stared in horror at the scene before them.

"Gabby…" Sal uttered.

He fumbled to Gabby's side, hands hovering over her corpse. Sal seemed conflicted in his emotions, perhaps both wanting to embrace his sister and being fearful of botching her body further. So instead, he trembled and gently caressed her cheek with the back of his hand. His tears dripped onto her maimed visage.

Xander, still panting from the scuffle, looked at Alison with a mixture of shock and gratitude. Then he turned to Sal, suffocated by guilt.

"Sal…"

Alison turned her palms upward, looking at herself in a new light. In her eyes, she was gazing at the hands of a murderer. It didn't matter if Gabby had died once before—she was family.

Xander approached Sal and put a hand on his shoulder. But Sal lurched his shoulder back, scuffing Xander off him.

"You did what you had to do." Sal used his knee as leverage to push himself up. "It's not the first time I've seen her die today."

Sal's words hung heavy in the air, the weight of his sorrow compressing the trio and making them physically weak. The salt of their tears was cumulatively palpable, mixing with the mustiness of the basement. It was humid.

A crash of glass upstairs broke the silence between them, followed by more gunshots from the outside and screaming.

***

They froze their movements, alert and waiting for the next sounds. When no footsteps followed, they released a collective sigh of relief. Each of the friends shared worried glances and nods, dispersing to find gear and weapons for protection. Sal rummaged through some boxes nearing the front of the hoard.

"This is my dad's hunting stuff. He didn't use it much. Bought it when your dad took him hunting two winters ago."

Sal pulled out a complex-looking bow. It was sleek black and half the size of him. The bowstring wrapped around the limbs of it several times over, far different, Sal said, from the recurve he was familiar with.

"Do you know how to use that?" Alison asked.

"Yeah…I've seen Dad handle it a few times at the range."

Sal tried to pull the string back and position the bow, but it took immense strength, and he struggled. Then he realized he was missing something.

"Arrows," he said. "Help me look around in these boxes."

Sal set the bow down gently on the concrete and combed through his dad's junk. Alison joined in to help. Xander, on the other hand, decided to look around the rest of the basement. Sal's family hadn't been hoarders, just his mom. But at least it was an organized mess.

Each box had neat labels, thanks to the label maker Miguel had gotten her for Christmas a few years back. The tags had kids' names, ages, and coordinating memories, like: "EDDY, 7, THANKSGIVING PARADE" and "MIGUEL, 15, NATIONAL ART HONOR SOCIETY." All of those memories were trapped in boxes, left to rot and be forgotten until someone needed something in the basement, passed by a box, and maybe, just maybe, had a faint flicker of recall.

Xander stopped when he noticed his name on one of the containers: "SAL & XANDER, 10/11, HALLOWEEN." He moved the boxes on top over and unfolded the flaps. That had been the year they were obsessed with Ghostface. And the best part about the theme was, they didn't have to choose who got to be the bad guy—Billy and Stu had both been it.

Xander pulled out the paper-thin black cloaks and couldn't help but smile. He pushed aside the signature white masks and even shoved away some old candy, which still looked eerily fresh. The plastic knives rested in the bottom of the box.

Their blades were clear plastic vessels containing a mess of fake blood. It dripped toward the handle when Xander picked one up. He dropped the knife when he took a blunder to the shoulder.

"Stop fucking around, Xander!"

It was Alison.

Xander spun around, clutching his shoulder where she had smacked him. "I wasn't—"

"No time for nostalgia," Alison snapped. "We need to be ready for whatever's out there."

Sal looked up from his search, the strain on his face visible. He fought to control his emotions. "Xander, help gather supplies. Why don't you go upstairs and fill this with food?"

Alison shoved a backpack into Xander's chest with force, knocking the wind out of him. She held up a quiver of arrows in her other hand and shook them like a box of treats before slinging the strap over her shoulder.

"These won't last long," she said. Then her voice turned into a whisper. "Not to mention, I don't think Sal knows what he's doing. I'll stay back and see what else we can find. Maybe try and get into the gun safe."

Xander sighed and returned the cloaks and items to the box.

"Sorry, just…got caught up in the memories."

"Yeah, well, memories won't keep us alive," Alison said, her voice softer now. "Let's focus."

Sal put a hand over Alison's shoulder. "Thanks, Allie. I'll take those, if you don't mind."

She shrugged Sal off her, took the strap, and put it around him instead. "Knock yourself out. But me and Xander still need something."

"I'm heading upstairs," Xander said.

"What do you mean? I can protect you," Sal replied.

Alison rolled her eyes. "Show me your dad's gun safe. I want to try and break in."

"Doubtful. That thing is a beast of a safe. You're not breaking in without a passcode."

"Well, we only have so many birthdays and anniversaries to go through. Come on."

Meanwhile, Xander climbed up the stairs, tasked with filling the bag Alison had thrown at him with the essentials. He pondered what that could be, sifting through the snack cupboard and tossing in some fruit snacks, Cheezerz Crackers, and chocolate and cream sandwich cookies. They were off-brand but tasted the same as the originals.

Xander tore open the sleeve and popped one of the imposters in his mouth before sealing it back up and throwing it in the backpack. There wasn't a lot of room left. He filled it with more snacks and added in some water bottles. Xander zipped up the bag and threw it over his shoulder, but the weight made him arch forward.

Cords zigzagged around the living room from the TV to the couch, under Sal's mom, and over the coffee table. Someone had been playing video games that day. Old PlayStation 2 controllers were plugged in, and an array of classic games had been spread out on the table. Xander wandered over and picked up an empty case of *Devil May Cry*.

He recalled the many hours spent on that game at Sal's. Xander appreciated all the old games his friend had and was jealous. Sal, on the other hand, had just wanted all the new stuff at Xander's house. Xander had the superior gaming PC, while Sal's dad had given his son a used Dell from his job.

A dust-coated Gameboy SP rested on the table. Xander wiped it down and took out the game from the slot—an old copy of *Doom*. Instinctively, he blew into the cartridge and into the game slot before popping the game back in. Xander grabbed the charger and shoved the Gameboy and the cord into the bag, zipping it back up afterward.

He plopped the bag on the kitchen counter and continued to look around. His hands hovered over the knife block. He unsheathed the chef's knife with caution, the recent image of the sword in Gabby's head still fresh in his mind. His fingers curled away and dropped the knife on the counter.

A loud thud came from the living room.

Xander warily looked over. A zombie had become tangled in the curtains, and shards of glass protruding from the window pierced its leathery skin. Its feet stomped and crunched on the broken pieces from earlier while it struggled to get free. It chomped its teeth together and whimpered a pathetic moan. With the torn and ragged clothes and clumps of bloody, matted hair, Xander didn't recognize her at first.

It was Mrs. Galzoni, his math teacher.

The enormous rock on her finger shined like a prism against the dying daylight of the setting sun. Every student who had taken her class had a hard-on for her. Even the girls envied her beauty. His friend Cheyenne—Shy—was vibrantly gay, and she would joke Mrs. Galzoni had turned her.

With her being trapped, it gave Xander time to really examine this sickness.

Maybe Sal was right. His teacher *looked* like a zombie. Growled like a zombie. Had a taste for human flesh and could only be killed via headshot. Real life just wasn't cinematic. The corpses were fresh. She didn't have gaping wounds and severed limbs. Mrs. Galzoni still looked very much human, aside from her mannerisms.

Anxiety coiled around Xander. He approached his teacher, though he was riddled with more curiosity than he was fear. As Xander neared, the zombie grew more excitable. She hastily clawed at the air, desperate to rip him to pieces.

Cheeks, being the friendly cat he was, ran up to the new visitor. The cat arched his back and rubbed his side against the zombie's leg, which only made matters worse. Mrs. Galzoni went completely hostile. The curtains were ripping while she ran in place, snapping at Xander and Cheeks.

Startled, the tabby scampered away.

The zombie's howling and rumbling halted when a bullet blasted through her forehead. It had been inches away from grazing Xander's cheek. His heart nearly stopped.

Xander cupped his ringing ears and winced in pain, turning to see Sal, who had been struggling to load an arrow into the bow. His jaw was agape, and the arrow slipped from his grasp, clanking to the floor. Next to him was Alison, clenching the grip of a .45, arms straight out and focus unbroken.

Alison finally removed her finger from the trigger and slumped her shoulders.

"What?" she asked, eyes darting between the boys. "I watch a lot of crime TV."

She holstered the gun, sliding it into the waistband of her jeans.

CHAPTER 5

"Got room for bullets in there?" Sal asked.

He set down the bow and put the loose arrow back in its quiver. In his deep pockets were boxes of ammo. The bullets jingled when Sal slapped them on the counter.

"Uhhh, not really," Xander said.

He took the bag and shook its contents, showing Sal it was full.

"I'm carrying the gun, so I'll carry the bullets," Alison chimed in.

"Why do *you* get the gun?" Xander asked.

Alison responded with a glare. After a pause, Xander nodded.

"Okay, fine. I see your point," he said. "Then, what weapon did you find me? I'm not exactly built to punch faces in."

Sal looked around, empty-handed. He scooped up the baseball bat he had dropped earlier and gave it a spin, inspecting the gore stuck to its metal, covering the faded writing. Sal ran it to the kitchen sink and let the jellied guts from his family swirl down the drain. Using a paper towel, he dried off the excess red-tinted water.

"This is perfect." Sal handed the bat to Xander, who was reluctant to take it.

"I'm going to be sick," Xander said.

He turned to catch the vomit trickling up his esophagus, swallowing it just in time. The first thing he focused on after was Abuela's bashed-in face, and his insides turned again. That time, it was harder to swallow. Xander's cheeks puffed out, his face shades of green. He was clearly unwell.

"Suck it up," Alison said. She grabbed the bat and rammed it into Xander's chest.

Sal's gaze wandered over to his mother and grandmother, who were still motionless in the living room. Next to them, his math teacher had a bullet-sized hole in her head. He looked toward the basement door, obviously thinking of Gabby. He shuddered but seemed too scared to cry. His legs shook, and his jaw chattered.

Alison put a hand on Sal's back to comfort him.

"We have supplies. Let's get out of here," she said. "Find somewhere else to go for the night."

Sal raided the foyer closet for shoes Alison and Xander could borrow. Xander had huge feet for his age, so Sal let Xander have one of the twins' tennis shoes. Luckily, Alison fit into his mom's shoes.

The trio peeked cautiously through the broken window of the living room, avoiding the math teacher's corpse, careful not to step on broken shards. The street was eerily quiet, aside from a burst fire hydrant spraying water a few houses down. Fatigued from the chaos of the day, the sun dipped below the horizon, casting long shadows across the desolate neighborhood. The ritzy suburban street was now a dystopian desert of abandoned cars, shattered windows, and the occasional shuffling figure in the distance, out of sight and earshot. The screams of before had simmered with the setting sun.

"Looks clear," said Xander.

He was the first to reach for the door handle, eager to escape the massacre of the people he had cared for. It creaked open. Nervous the undead would hear, Xander shimmied the door up and over, eliminating the noise of the loose hinges.

The group stayed close to the house while they walked down the sidewalk, backs to the bushes. There were undead across the street, wandering stragglers with their heads down, limping forward aimlessly, though they were sparse.

It was apparent there were still living people besides the teenagers, since there were beady eyes poking through the blinds of the neighboring houses. Some quickly retracted when one from the group met their glance—a poor attempt to conceal themselves. The symphony of shushing went well with the crescendo of chirping crickets, taking place of the cicadas winding down in the treetops.

"Over there," Sal said.

He pointed to a For Sale sign a few houses down. A picture of a plump realtor smiled on the sign. A red extension advertising an open house today flapped in the wind. The group jogged to it. Xander's asthma bothered him a little, but he didn't complain. Wheezing in the dry air made him cough, though it sounded more like a bark.

"Wait," Alison said. "Before we barge in, what if it's occupied? We need to be prepared. Draw out your weapons."

"Old man George died months ago. No one lives here. His kids came from down south for a weekend to throw out his stuff, smack up this sign, and leave," Sal noted.

"That's sad," said Xander. "But Alison is right."

Xander steadied the baseball bat in his hands, smacking the end lightly in his palm. He had played Little League in second grade because his father had wanted to raise a man, and in Aaron's eyes, you were a sissy if you didn't play sports. Sal had been in Little League, so that's the sport Xander chose too, to appease his father. He tried it for a summer and was consistent for a while, but Xander stopped showing up when he spent more time on a bench than on the field.

Alison had her hand on the pistol and the other on the doorknob. She looked to the boys. Without the pressure of surprise, Sal was able to load in the arrow with ease this time. He nodded and took a step back, glancing around them before aiming at the door. Xander had both hands on the bat.

Alison quickly pushed open the door, and it flung against the wall of the foyer. With haste, she pulled out the pistol and aimed.

"You go first, Xander," she said. "I don't want to shoot unless I have to. We don't need to bring attention to us here."

Without words, Xander swiveled around her and tiptoed through the entryway. The scent of orange floor cleaner hit him in the face. The hardwood shined with the fresh coat of oil against the dim lights of the streetlamps and the setting sun outside.

There were no pieces of furniture or boxes or anything, except a welcome mat on the stoop. An arrangement of flowers, cookies, and cursive invitations had been set on the half-wall peeking into the kitchen. A veil of darkness shrouded the upstairs.

On the other side of the staircase, Alison found the door to the basement. She opened it and turned on the light. When there were no sounds, she closed the door. Sal grabbed a cookie and left a trail of crumbs. His shoulders relaxed, and the bow swung at his sides while he explored the rest of the house. Xander found a bathroom.

"Finally, a moment to take a piss," he said.

"I think it's all clear! This place is empty," Alison echoed.

"I'll lock up," Sal said.

Xander set his bat on the sink and flipped the lid of the toilet seat, letting the stream flow. With a deep sigh, he allowed his tight muscles to loosen. But before his bladder had emptied, there was a rustling in the shower curtains. Xander sprayed a bit of the seat with piss, some on the floor—a mockery to the whimsical "Please Be Neat And Wipe the Seat" sign hanging above the toilet.

"Fuck, fuck, fuck." Xander fumbled, zipping up his jeans. "Guys!" he yelled.

When Xander swung open the door, Alison and Sal were standing in his way, weapons at the ready. Sal approached first, bow drawn, with Alison right behind him, pistol in hand.

"What is it?" Alison whispered urgently, eyes darting around the room. "I don't see anything."

The shower curtains ruffled again.

Xander grabbed the bat off the counter and put his back to them, ready to whack whatever was concealed behind the opaque material. He raised his bat, rotating his wrists to steady himself. He stepped toward the tub.

Right when he was about to swing, it happened.

"Please don't hurt me!" a man pleaded.

Xander let the bat fall to his side and threw open the curtain.

It was the realtor. His puffy face was red and blotched with tears. He had curled up in his brown suit, cuddling a pair of scissors still clutched against his chest.

"I thought you were one of them." The realtor scrambled to his feet, hands trembling.

The kids eyeballed him carefully, keeping their distance.

"Did one of them touch you?" Sal asked.

"No. Heavens, no. Brad. Brad Montgomery." The realtor dropped the scissors in the porcelain tub and extended a sweaty palm for a handshake, but the kids didn't return the gesture. "Okay, then."

Brad picked up the scissors and put them in his pocket.

"Do you mind stepping back so I can get out of the tub?"

The kids complied with his request and backed up.

While Brad climbed out, he inspected the trio thoroughly, as if expecting one of them to turn at any moment. His eyes widened when he saw their weapons, but he maintained a calm demeanor.

"Are you alone?" Alison kept her pistol pointed at the floor, a steady grip on it in case she had to take a shot.

"Unfortunately," said Brad. "Do any of you…children…have a phone I could use? I have been trying to get ahold of my wife…Well…ex-wife," Brad trailed off. "Doesn't matter. One of you, please let me use your phone."

"Not gonna happen," said Sal.

Annoyance washed over Brad's expression.

"Come on, kids. Give me a goddamn phone."

"Calm down. None of our phones work," Alison said. "Towers must be damaged or something."

"Shit. Shit, shit, shit." Brad took his phone from his pocket and checked again. In frustration, he chucked the phone at the shower wall, and the screen shattered. He cursed under his breath, picking up the broken pieces.

The kids watched him, unsure what to do or say. After a moment, Brad let out a frustrated sigh and turned to face them.

"I'm sorry," he said, tiredness in his voice. "I didn't mean to snap at you. It's just…everything that's happened…it's been hard to deal with."

"It's okay." Alison lowered her pistol slightly. "We understand. We've all been through a lot. We just—"

"Ever since the divorce, Katie has been a cunt," Brad said. "The bitch slept with my coworker. *My* coworker. Should have been the other way around. And guess what?"

The kids quickly realized Brad's problems had nothing to do with the undead. He hadn't experienced what they had—the death, the terror. Brad continued, not letting them get any words in.

"*She*. My coworker is a *she*. A woman. Or hermaphrodite. I don't know. Can't say for sure *what* she is packing in there. But hey, we can't say that anymore, can we?"

"Shut the fuck up," Sal said. "Fuck. Do you have any clue what's going on out there? I just had to bash the brains in of my mom and grandma and watch a katana slice through my little sister and a bullet go through the head of my math teacher. I don't know what happened to their parents"—Sal pointed at Xander and Alison—"but I'm sure it's not that far off. And you're concerned with the most *stupid* bullshit. No wonder why your wife is leaving you. You're a mess. Cowering in a bathtub, crying about a breakup, while kids like us have to save the fucking world."

Brad recoiled at Sal's words, stunned into silence. The weight of their experiences hit him like a ton of bricks. His own problems were trivial in comparison. Brad observed the three teenagers—really looked at them for the first time—and seemed to recognize the pain and trauma etched into their young faces.

Sal bit his lip to hush himself from speaking further. Xander and Alison stared in awe at him.

Brad, whose jaw had dropped, was unable to articulate his words.

"I'll...I'll go." Brad pushed through the doorway, and the kids stepped aside.

Sal tossed the bow back over his shoulder and balled his fists up.

"I'll leave you to...to whatever it is you're doing. I won't bother you anymore." Brad made his way toward the front door.

The trio lurked behind to see him off on his departure. Xander spoke up, his voice surprisingly calm.

"Wait," he said.

Brad turned to face him, a glimmer of hope in his eyes.

"We can't let him go out there. Not empty-handed," said Xander.

Brad frowned. Perhaps he had been hoping he could stay. After hearing the kids' stories, maybe he was terrified of what he'd have to do.

"What exactly *is* going on?" Brad asked. "Do any of you actually know?"

"Zombies," Sal was quick to answer.

Brad furrowed his brows and paused before chuckling. "No, really. So, you have no idea?"

"*Night of the Living Dead*? *28 Days Later*? *Legion*?" Sal continued. "Have you ever even watched a zombie flick? This is the only reasonable answer. Fuck you for laughing, like I'm some cute little kid."

"Sal, cool it," said Alison, holding him back.

"He's serious," Xander added. "You haven't seen what's out there."

"I'm going to hop in my Civic and take my happy little ass back to the Motel 6 to find an adult who may know what's going on," said Brad. "*Ha*. Zombies. Kids."

"Just let him go," said Alison. "We can't be babysitting. We have to survive. This guy will just weigh us down…literally."

"*Ha, ha*. A fat joke. Haven't heard those before." Brad opened the door, revealing the insidiously quiet neighborhood. He took out his keys to unlock his car but noticed the driveway was empty. "My car…My car!"

Brad waddled out to where his Honda should have been. Tire streaks lined the driveway, indicating it had likely been stolen.

"Not surprised," murmured Xander.

"Motel 6 is right down the road," said Sal. "I'll walk you there."

Xander shot Sal a surprised look.

"Really?" asked Brad.

"I'll go with you." Alison threw her arms up and slapped the pistol on her thigh. "Like hell are you going alone."

"I'll stay back. Search the rest of the house and keep guard. You got this?" Xander looked to Sal, who nodded in approval.

"Good plan," Sal agreed.

"T-thank you," said Brad. "You know you don't have to—"

"Shut up before I change my mind."

***

Sal and Alison escorted Brad down the street toward the motel. The neighborhood seemed to hold its breath. The silence was bizzare, broken only by the occasional distant groan or shuffle of the undead. Brad walked nervously between the two teenagers, clutching the pair of scissors and his broken phone, glancing around anxiously.

Sal paused and loaded up an arrow. There was an undead in the near distance, shuffling along their path. He lined up his sight and missed his first shot. Sal took a second arrow, and the zombie went down.

"Yes! Got'em." Sal balled his fist in excitement. "Did you see that, Alison? Second try."

Brad snapped back, his eyes wide. He turned to Sal.

"You just shot a man…"

"He was already dead. We've been trying to tell you what's going on, but you wouldn't listen," said Alison.

Sal grabbed his loose arrow from the sidewalk and, a few steps later, stomped on the corpse he had shot, tugging the arrow. After a few yanks, it pulled free from his skull.

The flickering neon sign of the motel came into view, casting an ominous glow over the deserted parking lot. Brad shuddered, exposed and vulnerable. Sal and Alison kept their weapons ready, scanning the area for any sign of danger.

The town was mostly gentrified and rich, except the few families who had been there since before the wave of people with money. A lot of the impoverished had fled to neighboring cities. A few from the old redlight district and established gangs had stuck around the Motel 6, along with businessmen looking for a good time away from their wives.

One of those men shot out of Room 1 when the group neared the motel.

"Please, help me!" The naked man screamed and ran toward them, penis flopping between his legs.

A woman who was scarcely dressed chased after, leaping on him like a predator seizing its prey. She took a bite out of his carotid and pulled the flesh into her mouth, like she were slurping up ramen noodles. Blood spurted everywhere, and the man fell to his knees. His screams turned into gurgles when he could no longer speak. Desperation filled his eyes, and he reached out for help.

Alison shot the hooker in the face while the man convulsed on the ground, slowly bleeding out. His hand fell to his side, and the whites of his bloodshot eyes twitched. Alison took a second shot at the man. He stopped trembling.

"We have to move." Alison kept her gun out and ready.

Sal put his back to hers, looking around the perimeter.

"Okay, let's get back to our base," Sal said.

"Wait!" Brad objected. "You're just leaving me here?"

"That's the plan."

Sal was already making his way back to the house, when the groans of the undead echoed in the air, triggered by the gunshots. Alison just shook her head at Brad and frowned. She trotted after her friend.

***

Brad fumbled with the key to his motel room, his hands shaking uncontrollably. He cursed under his breath, trying to calm himself. Finally, he managed to get the key in the lock but couldn't turn it.

The door was already unlocked.

Brad held his breath and pushed open the door to Room 3.

A dingy light hung over the center of the room, casting shadows in the corners. The bed had been neatly made, with mostly white linen. Fresh towels and miniature toiletries were on the nightstand. An air freshener puffed a cloud of lavender mist, startling Brad. He put his hands to his heart, which had skipped a beat.

Without a phone, the next way to find out what was going on was television. The motel still used cable, so there was hope of him watching the news. However, when Brad turned on the TV, he was greeted with a blaring alert for the emergency broadcast system. The volume on the TV was extremely loud, so he immediately turned it off.

But it was too late.

The noise had attracted a crowd. Groans sounded from nearby in adjacent rooms. Objects crashed to the floor, and multiple entities rustled beyond the paper-thin walls. There was an old landline on an otherwise empty desk next to the TV. He decided to try that next.

Brad picked up the phone off the receiver. It had a dial tone. Finally, something was going right. He thought about who to call, pondering for a moment, when he realized he never memorized anyone's number anymore. Brad took out his cell, testing the touch screen to see if it still worked through the shattered glass. It was intermittent, but with some fidgeting, he was able to navigate to his contact list.

His first thought was to try Katie. He referenced her number from his cell, but it went straight to voicemail. The house there didn't have a landline. Maybe that was the reason the call wouldn't go through—cell towers were down, but landlines still worked.

"But who still has a landline besides this shitty motel," Brad mumbled to himself.

He slammed the phone against the receiver.

Brad slumped into the chair by the desk, running a hand through his thinning hair. It creaked when Brad shifted his weight, unable to sit still. The situation was beyond anything he could have imagined. Brad needed to think, to come up with a plan. He couldn't just stay in the motel room indefinitely, especially not with the sounds of the undead closing in on him.

Brad peeked through the half-open blinds. Shadows moved past the window, silhouettes of the undead shuffling aimlessly. Sal and Alison were disappearing into the distance, their figures growing smaller. He was alone, but not really, and he could only hold up in Room 3 for so long.

Suddenly, there was a loud thud against the door, followed by a throaty growl. Brad's heart raced, and he backed away. He needed to find a weapon. The scissors in his pocket seemed woefully inadequate now.

He frantically searched the room. The dresser drawers were empty, except for a *New Testament Bible* and dust-frosted crucifix. The bathroom yielded a flimsy toilet brush. His eyes fell on the mini fridge. Brad yanked it open.

A couple of beer bottles. Not much, but better than nothing. He deemed the crucifix his best option, inspecting its pointed ends. It was hefty for a motel cross, made of real wood and solid.

Another thud. The knob shifted, and the door opened. A terrified Brad, gripping the crucifix, froze in place.

A woman in a hotel uniform, now one of *them*, stumbled into the room, her eyes milky white. Her agape mouth revealed the clusters of flesh in her teeth and bloodied gums. Her nametag read: "Diana."

She lunged at him, and Brad swung the crucifix as hard as he could, the sharp points connecting with the zombie's head. However, it was too blunt to pierce the skull. What would have left a living person unconscious didn't faze Diana. The force of the blow sent the zombie staggering back, but she quickly recovered, twitching her head and cracking her neck. She purred a low, menacing growl.

Brad's mind raced. He needed to act quickly, so he swung the crucifix again, aiming lower this time. The sharp edges caught Diana in the throat, tearing through already decayed flesh. Blood and dark fluid sprayed, and the zombie seemed momentarily disoriented. Brad seized the opportunity, dropping the crucifix and grabbing one of the beer bottles from the mini fridge.

He smashed the bottle against the edge of the desk, creating a jagged weapon. The wheat-scented beer fizzed to the ground. When Diana lunged at him again, Brad drove the broken bottle into her eye socket with all his strength. The glass punctured deep, and Diana's body convulsed before collapsing to the floor.

Brad's breath came in ragged gasps. He kicked the door shut, but it was caught by grasping hands. There was a horde outside, wild and ravenous.

A bouquet of claws tore at Brad, ripping apart his clothes and exposing his jiggling flaps of skin. They clawed through his flesh with ease, and blood poured out of him.

Brad screamed.

***

"Do you think that was…?" Alison asked.

"If it is, it's too late," Sal replied. "We have to put us first. Us and Xander. We have to get back to him and make sure he's okay. We should have never escorted that prick anyway."

"I agree. But…I still feel bad. No one deserves this."

"*We* don't deserve this. Let's at least make the most of us being out and raid this gas station. Then we stay inside and wait for our phones to come back on again."

The Roadway Mart was a relic. It had been there longer than most of the housing. The city used to be what was called a "pass-through town"—not meant for stopping and touring, just a gateway to get to the major cities. Roadway Mart was the first mark on the map where truckers would stop and refuel their tankers and stomachs. Now, due to the congestion of corporate America traffic, truckers tended to avoid the route altogether, unless they had to make a delivery in the town itself.

Roadway's neon pink and blue open sign was always on, even if they closed by 11:00 p.m. It was old and ran hot, so the buzzing sound was extra apparent on quiet nights, but not tonight. When Sal and Alison moseyed up to the gas station, a group of people were already there. They threw something in the window, and the glass shattered, setting off the alarm.

"You fill up on snacks, and I'll grab the cash," one man said to another.

"Fucking cakewalk," the other man replied.

He clenched a handgun and darted through the empty storefront.

"We should go." Alison grabbed Sal by the shoulder and pulled him back.

The alarm blared through the neighborhood. The rising symphony of groans and hissing sprinted toward the noise.

"Those canned goods aren't going to last forever," said Sal.

He ran toward the gas station, bow in hand. With great reluctance, Alison followed, pistol ready.

One of the thugs stuck their mouth under the slush machine, letting the red icy mush overflow his lips, while the other was trying to hold up his sagging pants stuffed with cash.

"Who the fuck's there?"

Saggy Pants Man cocked his gun and search the Roadway. Sal didn't make any effort to hide. He was already stuffing his pockets with candy bars and jerky.

"We got kids, Lyric. Hurry the fuck up."

Lyric was the man binging on the cherry slush. He did a poor job of wiping his mouth, looking annoyed.

"Theo, what we care 'bout kids for?"

"Hurry, Sal," Alison urged. "They're coming."

She tugged at Sal to leave.

The undead poured onto the premises from every direction, lurking around abandoned cars and gas pumps. Mouths open, they clung to the flickering neon sign like a beacon. The alarm and the sounds from inside were a magnet, drawing the undead like moths to a flame.

Sal finally gave in and followed Alison. They ran outside and swiftly ducked behind a parked car upon seeing the army of undead. The two watched the looters raiding the store.

"Don't make any sudden movements," Sal whispered.

Alison nodded, her grip tightening on the pistol. They started to retreat slowly, aiming toward the back of the building. The friends attempted to keep low, skating their feet across the blacktop.

"On the count of three, we run," said Sal. "One."

A few stragglers wandered from the horde and got uncomfortably close to the kids. Sal held up two fingers and mouthed, *two*. Alison restrained herself from trembling.

A loud crash echoed from inside the gas station. Lyric had knocked over a display, sending a cascade of cans and bottles to the floor. The zombie nearing the kids snapped its head toward the thugs and ran forward, snarling, teeth snapping.

"Three!" Sal said.

The undead surged the Roadway, while Sal and Alison ran the opposite direction. Alison had to make an effort to not run too far ahead of Sal. She looked back just in time to watch the horde of zombies pour into the store. One of the men fired his gun wildly, but it was too late. The undead overwhelmed them. Their screams were cut short by the sound of tearing flesh.

The friends ran about halfway back to the house, when Sal motioned for Alison to stop so he could catch his breath.

"Hold up," he said. "I need to make a stop."

Sal slowed his pace next to a construction zone on a new commercial lot. There were excavators and steamrollers parked and abandoned, keys still in the ignitions. Big mounds of dirt had tread marks all over, and there was a port-a-potty on the edge of the mud near the road.

"We need to get back to Xander," said Alison. "No more raids."

"No, no, no…None of that." Sal took a deep breath. "Just give me a minute."

"No." Alison was stern.

"Ali…" Sal said. "I have to shit. Give me a goddamn minute."

Alison's face flushed, and for the first time since they had ventured out, she tucked her pistol in her jeans. She couldn't make eye contact with Sal.

"Hurry up," she said. "I'll guard your ass, I guess."

Alison kicked pebbles around the construction site. When Sal began grunting, she chuckled and made greater distance between them so she didn't have to listen. Moments later, car tires squealed, and someone began screaming.

Down the road, a woman was trapped in her car and being overrun by zombies.

Alison bit her lip, conflicted between desire to help the stranger but not wanting to leave Sal. And more importantly, there were many more of *them* than there was of her. She was one girl with a gun.

Alison's nerves got the better of her. She quivered, reaching for one of the boxes of bullets in her pockets. A few golden pieces clanked to the ground. Too scared to look away, she didn't bother picking them up.

She counted one by one, loading seven bullets in the magazine and walking toward the cluster of chaos. Alison tried to see if she could make out the number of undead.

In a whisper, she continued, "One…two…three…"

The window on the car door started to crack. It formed a web of lines before the glass gave in and shattered.

"Seven, eight…"

Alison froze. She held the gun out toward the mess of undead but couldn't do it. She was too scared.

The woman was being torn out of the vehicle. It was too late. Her screams soon turned into nothing. But Alison kept her eyes peeled on the gruesome scene.

She saw someone she recognized.

Her lips pouted and shuddered, holding back a wail.

"Mom…"

CHAPTER 6

Evelyn pivoted, her movements still clumsy and uncoordinated. She weaved in and out of the soft warmth of the streetlamps coming on one by one when she passed. The light waned, and a shadowy figure emerged. The metallic sheen of a pistol's barrel reflected the fading glow.

The figure was a woman. No, a child…And as Evelyn's vision cleared, recognition hit her hard.

"M-Mom? Is that you?"

Evelyn tried to speak, but only a low groan escaped her lips. She raised a hand, hoping to convey some semblance of communication. In response, Alison's grip on the pistol tightened, and her finger moved toward the trigger. Tears streamed down Alison's face, and she took a step back.

"Please, don't make me do this," Alison said. "I don't want to hurt you, but I will if I have to."

Evelyn slowly moved forward, fighting against the urge to attack. Alison couldn't hurt her. She focused on the memories of her children, who anchored her humanity, or what was left of it. Something pecked inside her, making her feel different.

She pointed her hand to where her heart used to beat, hoping her daughter would understand. The more Evelyn pushed herself to move, the more the urges inside of her began to surface. Her impulses had other plans. Evelyn struggled to defy the gnawing hunger within her.

Alison seemed to hesitate, her eyes searching the corpse's face for any sign of her mother.

"Mom, if you're still in there, you have to fight it. Please, come back. I need you, and I'm scared."

When Alison said this, Evelyn's heart throbbed. A guttural growl escaped Evelyn's throat in place of what she was dying to say: *I love you.* She forced herself to take another step forward, her arm outstretched.

Alison's tears flowed freely now, and she lowered the pistol, taking a shaky breath.

"I love you, Mom. I'm sorry I ran. I was so scared."

Evelyn's body fought against the smile twitching on her face. For a moment, the world around them disappeared, and it was just the two of them—mother and daughter, reunited.

But the hunger inside Evelyn grew.

The peace was short-lived. A deep roar echoed through the street, and Evelyn snapped her head toward it. The horde had noticed them, drawn by the scent of fresh blood and the sound of Alison's voice. They lumbered toward Alison, their eyes vacant and hungry.

The oncoming frenzy made something snap in Evelyn. The little light in the back of her head was snuffed, and a feral energy took over. She took a swipe at her daughter.

Alison jumped back just in time and screamed. She raised her pistol and got a shot off.

Alison missed.

***

There were too many of them. She had to turn back. Alison was overcome by a sense of pity for leaving her mother with the horde of monsters, unwilling to accept she was one of them. Despite Evelyn swiping at her, Alison felt something different, and it pained her heart. But she didn't have time to ponder over what that sensation was.

Alison had to run back to Xander without drawing attention to their temporary homestead.

She had to get Sal and get back. Alison couldn't lose them too.

Sal emerged from the port-a-potty, adjusting his belt and looking annoyed.

"What the hell are you doing, Alison? Get away from there!"

Alison didn't respond. Her eyes locked on her mother's empty shell.

Something about Evelyn had changed. Her milky eyes met Alison's, and for a moment, recognition flickered in their depths, though it quickly faded. The other zombies were closing distance.

Alison's voice was barely more than a whisper.

"Sal, it's my mom. She's…she's one of them."

Evelyn took another swipe at her, but Alison dodged again.

"Alison. We have to go. Now," Sal demanded.

"No!" Tears streamed down her face. "She's still my mom. She recognizes me."

Sal shook his head, pulling at Alison's arm. "Your mom is dead. We have to leave, or we'll end up like her. Is that what you want? Is that what your mom would have wanted?"

Evelyn's movements were staggered, but she seemed determined. And hungry. Her eyes fixed on Alison. The other zombies were no longer distracted by the easy prey in the car. They had gobbled that poor woman up, aside from her bones, and some were licking those clean.

Finally, Alison gave in. Her resolve wavered because he was right. She had to protect Sal and her brother. That's what Mom would have wanted.

With a last, heartbroken look at her mother, Alison turned and ran with Sal, her tears blurring her vision. They sprinted down the road, away from the construction site, their footsteps echoing in the deserted streets.

Sal's tone became cold and callous.

"You should have put her out of her misery."

They ran, retracing their steps, moving through alleys and side streets to avoid the larger groups of the monsters.

The homeless man who used to panhandle at the side of the freeway lunged for Alison, and she almost tripped. His eyes were glassed over, and he hissed. Sal helped Alison shake free by curb-stomping him in the face right when the man was about to nip her leg. The town had become a twisted labyrinth of horror, but Alison's willpower to survive fueled her every step.

They neared their safe house, and the sounds of the undead grew fainter. The two of them burst through the door, slamming it shut behind them and bolting it securely.

Xander looked up from his mindless pacing, his face lighting up with relief.

"You're back!" he exclaimed, rushing over to hug Alison.

She embraced her brother tightly, her heart aching with the weight of what she had seen. "Yeah, we're back," she said, her voice cracking.

Sal dropped the bag of supplies on the table, his face grim.

"We need to talk."

Xander frowned.

"What happened out there?"

Alison took a deep breath, bracing herself.

"We saw Mom. She…she's one of them now."

***

Xander's face crumpled with grief. He didn't hesitate to cling to his sister, sobbing. Xander stroked Alison's blond strands out of her face and wiped her tears. His own fell down his cheek. She smelled rancid, like one of *them*. Her hair was greasy and drenched in sweat, her clothes coated with blood.

"I figured we would run into her again, eventually…But not so soon."

***

Sal let the siblings comfort each other. He put his back to them and faced the window. But he wasn't looking out. Instead, he peered at his own reflection. Sal thought to himself how much he looked like his father then and wondered if he was okay.

***

The kids prepared to tuck in for the night, but Alison couldn't shake the image of her mother's lifeless eyes. Regret washed over her for not putting her mom out of her misery, like Sal had said. No matter what, she would protect her brother and honor her mother's memory. Even if that meant facing the undead version of her mother in the future.

Sleep became foreign to the kids. They took turns keeping watch on the house, but none of them slept. Xander stared at the ceiling, listening to every sound outside and trying to diagnose how close they were. Alison lay in a corner by herself, wondering the same thing but less hopeful they would make it through the night.

***

Sal had his back to the wall and watched the others, eyes drooping, waiting for his shift to be done. His stomach growled.

He got up and shuffled to the half-wall to grab a cookie from the open house display, but there were none left. Sal licked his fingers and dabbed the plate to pick up the crumbs, smacking his lips. He unloaded the candy bars and beef jerky he had taken from the Roadway onto the kitchen counter, organizing them by color and size.

Sal was a big snacker, but he was definitely missing his mother's cooking. She had made the best enchiladas. His mother would stuff them to the brim with cheese, then coat them in a secret sauce neither she nor Abuela ever disclosed. And now he would never know.

He decided to go through the backpack to probe what Xander had grabbed. Sal expected canned goods and general survival items, but Xander must have had the same cravings. Only junk food. Sal emptied the contents with the rest of the goodies and began to organize.

A few other items that weren't food surprised Sal. His gameboy toppled onto the trophy of treats, along with the charger. His disappointment of food choices was soon forgotten when he booted up his saved file of *Doom*. He grabbed some cookies and plugged in the charger, switching on the GBA. The 8-bit music wasn't loud, but it was the only sound in the house, other than Sal munching on his snack.

"Sal, can you please turn that off? You're going to attract them with the noise," Alison murmured, obviously irritated.

But Sal persisted, and fight music commenced. He mashed buttons, shooting aliens and traveling through the pixelated universe, oblivious to the world around him. When his health was running low in the midst of battle, he shut the gameboy and tossed it aside.

"Xander, it's your turn to keep watch," he said.

***

Alison's nerves were frayed from the endless tension. Sal's carefree attitude grated on her, but she tried to focus on their immediate survival.

Xander stood up, rubbing his tired eyes and nodding. He took his place by the window, peering through the blinds at the dark, zombie-infested streets.

"There's so many more than there were earlier. Do you think this is happening everywhere?"

"I sure as hell hope not." Sal lay down on the hardwood floor.

Eventually, Sal and Alison got some sleep, even it was barely two hours. At least it was something.

***

Xander nodded off, leaning against the wall. He had dozed a few times and woken himself up by his own snoring. The sun's rays made him squint. He was awake for good this time.

Alison put her hand on his shoulder, startling him.

"Jeez, Allie. You scared the crap out of me."

"Sorry, but you should lay down," she said. "After you nap a few, we'll get going."

"Going where?"

Sal joined in the circle. "Anywhere but here. This place is empty. We're like sitting ducks, and we only have food that will last a few days, with no other supplies."

Xander went over to the faucet and turned it on, cupping his hands under the tap to rinse off his face and drink from his palms.

"I suppose you have a point." He wiped his face and ran his fingers through his hair.

"Any ideas on where to go?" Alison asked.

Sal leaned back, thinking. "Downtown will be infested. All of the boutiques and bars are instantly ruled out."

"There's an old mall on the outskirts of town," Alison noted. "It's been abandoned for years, but it might have some stuff left. It's spacious and not at all near downtown. It's perfect."

"Like hell it is," Xander objected. "No way."

"My man, I'm disappointed in you," Sal said. "You haven't made your sister watch any of the classics, have you?"

Alison snapped.

"Well, I don't hear anyone else with a grand plan. Come on. Anyone?"

"Cut it out, Allie. The mall is a terrible idea. Trust me," said Xander.

Alison folded her arms and pouted, storming off in the other direction.

The group hadn't strayed much from the living room. Even when Xander had been there by himself and was tasked to explore, he had stayed clear of the basement. With Gabby and all, it was too reminiscent.

Xander spoke up. "What about the planetarium?"

"Wouldn't be anything useful in there," Alison said. "What about Fit Freakz?"

"The muscle-head gym by that vegan restaurant?" Sal asked.

"Yes, that one. And, hey. I go to that gym. It's not all big dudes, you know."

"What do you need a gym for? You're in high school."

"I train." Alison rolled her eyes. "Look. There's showers, lockers, a Freshies, luxury…It's got everything. And it's easy to hold off. There's only one entrance and the back door."

"Still not a place with anything useful, in my opinion. What about food?" asked Xander.

"Freshies is a cafe. Duh."

"What do they sell? Muscle Milk and rabbit food?" Sal laughed.

"They have a whole kitchen. It's a local gig that does farm-to-table to-go. You've seen those food trucks around, right? Yeah, they have protein shakes too. But there's a whole bunch of stuff. And it wouldn't kill you two to get in better shape."

"Okay, Allie. You convinced us. We were just poking fun. Let's pack up." Xander looked out the window one last time. "The crowd has thinned out. I only count four I can see out there right now. Last night, counted maybe a hundred."

***

Xander was the designated backpack carrier. He swung the baseball bat alongside his legs while they walked.

"Man, we really need a car," Sal said. "Why don't we go back to your place and grab your mom's Expedition?"

"Why not your dad's Toyota?" Xander asked.

"What do you think would win in a zombie apocalypse: a Ford Expedition or a Toyota Corolla?"

"Neither," said Alison. "After watching those things overrun that poor woman in her car…I don't want to be in one. I feel safer on foot."

"Says the track star. The Expedition is at the shop anyway. It makes a noise or a squeak, and Mom freaks out and takes it in for service," Xander said.

Sal sighed. "How about the minivan? Dad was going to spruce it up and give it to Miguel and Eddy for their birthday, but it's just sitting in the driveway. It stands a better chance of protection than the Corolla."

CHAPTER 7

Evelyn watched her prey grow smaller and smaller in the distance, but she led the horde onward toward Alison and Sal until she no longer saw them at all. When they were out of sight, they were also too far for her other senses. She could no longer hear them, smell their meat. Instead, Evelyn was left with the faint scent of peaches from her daughter's perfume.

The hunter's instinct washed away, and she stood still. The horde scattered around her at this point. Without their senses leading instincts, they aimlessly wandered around the neighborhood, but not Evelyn. She was burdened by humanity. A single tear rolled down her cheek.

Evelyn found more control over her motor skills under the light of the moon. She didn't bother understanding why; it was just true. Evelyn stretched her fingers and clenched her hands into fists. She was angry. But she felt nothing when digging her nails into her own flesh. There was no pain or sense of touch. It was like she were a ghost, just passing through time and space, left to wander a world with no room for her in it.

She looked at the other undead. A few were sniffing around the car they had collectively pulled the woman out of, searching for more meat. Evelyn reached out and touched a man's shoulder. The monster swung around, and his jaw unlatched. The mandible barely hung onto the rest of his face.

It took a moment, but Evelyn recognized him as her mailman.

She tried to communicate with him, but even with her new sense of power at nightfall, she couldn't form words. Only growls and wheezing came out of her mouth, while the words she wanted to say pulsed in her brain. It hurt to think. Evelyn was exhausted, just trying to muster up the energy to form a sentence. She pressed over and over again in her thoughts: *Can you understand me?*

It couldn't understand her. The former mailman gazed through Evelyn, hardly giving her an up and down. When he realized she wasn't edible, he turned his cheek and went back to combing the car for human scraps.

The mailman, a fragment of Evelyn's former life, had been reduced to a mindless, ravenous beast. The pain of being trapped in her own decaying body, unable to communicate or protect her children, gnawed at her. Despite the physical numbness, the emotional agony was all too real. Her thoughts were a chaotic whirlwind of memories, the remnants of her humanity clashing with the insatiable hunger of her new existence.

Carnal desires and images of ripping her kids apart and savoring their tender meat…Those were thoughts which both disgusted and excited Evelyn. She shook them from her head and wandered. With the torment of thought dissolved by aimless meandering, starvation returned, corroding her from the inside.

She spotted a pair of raccoons dismantling the dumpster of a fast food restaurant. When focusing in on the critters, Evelyn discovered a strange power. Their chittering whispers were not only audible, but loud. She could hear their tiny hearts pounding from yards away.

Curiosity propelled Evelyn toward the creatures. They paid her no mind when she neared them. Humans had never been a concern as predator. They probably sat outside the back door of places like this and begged for food—teenagers bringing them scraps of nuggets and french fries.

One of them peered up with its beady black eyes, gnawing on a fry. The glare of the streetlights made their eyes glow.

A hissing noise escaped Evelyn's mouth. It watered for sustenance. She thought maybe these raccoons would calm her hunger. Part of her shuddered at the thought. The old Evelyn would never have considered eating an adorable little guy like that. But the new one was desperate. And the smell of discarded grease she used to love repulsed her.

The raccoon still watched Evelyn, grabbing fries one by one, like he were watching a show. The other clawed at an unopened bag, chittering to its friend. In one swift motion, Evelyn snatched the raccoon by the scruff. It was plump and fierce. The raccoon made all sorts of noises and clawed at her arm, biting her in an attempt to escape. But Evelyn's nails dug deep.

She didn't feel anything. The fresh wounds barely even bled anymore. Her heart wasn't beating to pump the blood through. She was decaying at a rapid pace, and deep down, Evelyn knew it went faster when she was hungry.

The critter screamed for help, but his friend scurried off without him. The raccoon's pudge shifted, and he tried to use his little feet to push away. Evelyn felt a pang of guilt, but just for a moment. She unhinged her jaw, fitting the entire head of the raccoon into her mouth. Evelyn chomped down, and the flesh squished.

Fur got stuck to her tongue and the roof of her mouth. It was annoying, trying to get to the meat of the animal. She crunched the skull like she were munching on a carrot. Sinew snapped in her mouth while she tried to chew through the tough pieces. She spit out shards of bone like popcorn kernels, just a minor inconvenience with her meal.

The raccoon didn't taste good, but it wasn't bad either. It was much more bearable when she chewed through to the brain. The texture was satisfying and easy to get down her throat. But it was missing something. The stomach area was vile, tasting like the trash it had been eating—fatty, greasy, junk food.

Hunger was still present, but it no longer pained Evelyn. After a few more bites of the creature, she cast it aside into the dumpster.

Restlessness plagued her, and she slumped against the side of the brick building. She closed her eyes, seeing only black. Evelyn tried to imagine her life before but couldn't.

A group of people conversed in the near distance. They weren't people like her. These were still alive.

"Shut up! You're going to get us killed."

"How could you! You just killed her! My girlfriend. You threw her to them. You're no better than them!"

"It was her or me. You would have done the same."

Evelyn focused on two men running up the street, undead chasing them. They both had knives. A trail of dead bodies had been left behind, including the fresh corpse of a girl. This was about a half-mile away, but Evelyn could sense them perfectly. Instead of moseying toward them, she hid in the shadows.

Other undead weren't as intelligent. As soon as they detected the fresh meat, they burst from their hiding places and chased the humans. But each time, they were met with a blade to the skull. Evelyn tucked herself in the foliage and waited for the boys to come her way. Unlike the helpless raccoons, the humans had an appetizing scent. Something throbbed within Evelyn the closer the two men came.

"Fuck, Stan. I'm sorry, okay? What do you want me to do? I can't take it back."

"An eye for an eye, how 'bout that!"

He pushed Stan.

"Is that really what you want? To kill me, Fred? Really?"

Fred pushed Stan again.

Evelyn had the jitters, excited her prey was walking right into her trap. She made herself invisible. Evelyn thought to hold her breath and chuckled, realizing she didn't have to do that anymore.

"I wouldn't mind fucking you up a little bit. That's for sure."

"Fine. If that will make you feel better." Stan's voice choked. "Go ahead. I can't keep doing this. Kill me. Fucking kill me, Fred. You don't have the balls. That's why Cassie blew me last week after practice."

This made Fred snap. He lunged at his friend and started wailing on him, toppling over and straddling Stan, punching his face relentlessly. The man on the ground was a blubbering mess, crying and not fighting back. Fred unsheathed his knife and raised it above his head with two shaking hands.

But when blood broke from the punches, Evelyn couldn't contain herself any longer. She pounced on top of Fred, and the knife dropped to the pavement.

Fred's screams echoed into the night when Evelyn's teeth sank into his shoulder, tearing through flesh and muscle. His body convulsed in pain, and he tried to push her away, but Evelyn's grip was unyielding. Fred was in shock.

"Stan, bud. Help me! You gotta help me!"

Blood spurted from Fred like a sprinkler. The taste of the warm crimson ignited a primal frenzy within Evelyn, drowning out the remnants of her humanity. She bit down on the man and tore his shoulder clean of meat, chewing his arm like Mickey Mouse devouring corn on the cob in a black and white classic. That's what it felt like too. She could practically hear the whistling in the back of her head while she savored every piece of the fresh delicacy.

Such bliss.

Fred's head fell limp to his other shoulder. The screaming and pleading ceased.

Stan, still lying on the ground in a mess of his own blood, stared in horror as the scene unfolded. He scrambled backward, trying to distance himself from Evelyn, but his limbs seemed uncooperative.

Evelyn clamped her jaws down on the back of Fred's neck, and with a final, brutal snap, she severed the cervical vertebrae from spinal column. If he wasn't dead before, he was now.

Evelyn was full, engorged even. But she couldn't stop. Gluttonous and insatiable, she ate. And the kid who had asked to die sat in horror, watching Evelyn feast on his friend. She was bloated. Evelyn couldn't consume much more, but she wanted to try.

She released Fred from her grip, and he slumped to the ground. The rest of his fluids pooled underneath him. Leisurely, Evelyn prowled toward Stan. He didn't bother to run, didn't even scream. When Evelyn locked onto his ankle, he just accepted his fate.

The lack of chase made this one taste worse.

After one bite, Evelyn pushed herself up. She growled at the man and then turned around, looking up at the moon. Evelyn basked in the light, taking in the energy and feeling herself heal.

The boy got up and scurried away, but only because she let him leave.

Evelyn turned around, watching him fade into the darkness with a mixture of relief and sorrow. She couldn't protect her children if she continued to give in to the monster inside her. Evelyn needed to find a way to control her urges, to hold on to whatever humanity she had left. But for now, this energy, this power, would help her carry on and hold onto herself a little longer.

I'm not dead yet, she thought.

Hissing came from around the corner. The raccoon that had run away was eating the remnants of his friend. With a belly full of trash, there was no way he was hungry. But Evelyn understood.

She went over to the creature. It had madness in its eyes, picking pieces of intestine from the dead raccoon. It quickly turned and hoarded its food, eyes on Evelyn.

Something was different about the creature. It was fearless. Hungry. It reminded her a lot of herself. It hissed, and Evelyn crouched on all fours, grunting since she couldn't speak. The creature sniffed around her, and their noses touched. Its whiskers brushed her cold skin. Then it went back to eating like she wasn't there.

Evelyn patted the raccoon on the head. It purred like a cat and relaxed.

Behind her was a gurgling sound.

The boy she had killed—*Fred, was it?*—convulsed and foamed from the mouth. Then he became still. His head rolled over, and he looked to Evelyn. The boy sat up, but his head flopped around on his neck from lack of support. It growled and raised its palms, inspecting its hands.

Like the raccoon, there was something different about this one. Evelyn sensed he was sentient, like her. Not like the other bumbling idiots. A feeling of motherhood returned. She had created this one. Thoughts of Xander and Alison dissipated now she had something new to look after.

Evelyn made a guttural groan and gurgled out to Fred. The boy obeyed and found his footing, limping his way toward his sire. She didn't need to say anything. They communicated through the limbo in their eyes.

Evelyn had used to believe in God. But as she stumbled in the direction of her old workplace, her minion toting behind her, she started to recall what had squandered her beliefs.

CHAPTER 8

Sunlight seeped into the dingy garage when Sal pushed up the door. The minivan was a mess. Dried mud had caked on like fireworks. It was burgundy and used to have a sparkle. Now it was covered in dust, and cobwebs extended from the side mirrors. Sal opened the driver side door and flipped down the visor. The keys fell onto the seat.

"Moment of truth," said Sal.

He put the keys into the ignition and attempted to start the van, but it wouldn't roll over. It heaved like an eighty-year-old smoker, struggling to start. He wiggled the steering wheel and tried two more times before poking his head out.

"No luck," said Sal.

"Do you think it's the battery?" asked Alison.

"I don't think it would turn over at all if it were the battery. The damn thing was trying. May be the alternator? I dunno. I watched my dad fix things sometimes. Moreso when I was little and he'd make me come to the garage and watch. But I don't think I learned anything other than Dad's favorite beer and how to match up a socket."

Sal lifted the hood but had no idea what he was looking at. Lucky for him, he noticed the battery had fallen loose from its tray. The wires were just yanked loose. He closed his eyes, trying to focus on the memory of his dad showing him how to change a battery in that same garage.

Mijo, pay attention, now. It's very important to not mix these wires up.

With concentration, Sal drew on these thoughts of his father and reattached the wires, making sure the battery was snug in its tray.

"Xander, try starting her up," he called out.

Xander put one foot in the driver's side and turned the key once more. Nothing. He tried again. The van boomed a big smoker's cough and sputtered. It was a rough start, but then it purred, happy to be brought back to life.

"Guys, hurry up. We got trouble coming."

Alison, who was standing watch, had a look of concern on her face.

"Take care of it. We trust you," said Sal.

"I can't handle this one by myself."

Sal grabbed the largest torque wrench he could find from his father's tool bench and a crowbar.

"Xander, go on and take lead," said Sal. "Alison, catch."

Sal ran up to Alison and tossed her the crowbar.

"Only shoot if we have to," he said.

Ten zombies had rolled up toward the house, their vacant eyes leading them blindly. They limped and staggered until the kids were spotted, then a flurry of whirling decay. Xander pushed Alison behind him.

He gripped the bat and started swinging. It took about two hits before the first zombie's face was smashed in, but Xander kept going. Guts splattered all over Alison. She pursed her lips in disgust and readied the crowbar, bracing herself.

But then Sal ran up behind Alison and whacked the wrench into the back of another zombie's head, who was inches away from biting his friend.

"Snap out of it, Xander. You're going to get bit!" Alison got her first kill from the horde after a few smacks of metal and a puncture through the eye socket.

Xander's primal senses seemed to have overcome him, and he recklessly ran into the group of zombies, bashing the steel bat into their skulls with an uncommon force. Five had been taken out already. Sal and Alison were only on their second kills, and Xander was clearly out of breath.

Through the hum of the undead growling and croaking, Xander was wheezing. Warrior-painted blood had been swiped across his face. He dropped the bat and grasped his chest.

Sal struggled with two zombies, while Alison was faced the other way, taking care of the last.

But one of the zombies they thought had been downed stirred. One eye hung by a single cord of flesh from its socket. The other was glassed over with a tinge of excitement. Flaps of skin rubbed together, spurting out blood from the undead's face. He eagerly snapped his jaws, inching closer to Xander. His cracked and dirty nails clawed into the pavement, yellow bile drooling from his mouth.

Xander stumbled back, his breath coming in ragged gasps. He grabbed the bat, continuing to hyperventilate.

Sal put down one of his two and shouted, "Xander! Look out!"

This got Alison's attention. She jerked her focus to her brother.

Without hesitation, Alison dropped the crowbar and whipped the gun from her jeans. She shot the zombie in the head and ran to Xander.

"You dumb fuck. Of all the things to pack, you forget an inhaler?"

"You're the dumb fuck," Xander wheezed. "You weren't supposed to shoot."

He slowly but surely caught his breath.

"Gabby had an inhaler. Let me grab hers. She won't need it anymore." Sal threw open the screen door and ran in the house.

"Also…Held up in the bathroom, escaping our dad trying to murder us…It wasn't my first thought."

***

Over the edge of the horizon, the harsh sun peeked, casting a mirage on the blacktop. More of them were coming. A *lot* more.

Alison tightened her grip on the pistol, scanning the silhouettes beginning to take shape.

Sal was quick, bursting back into the garage with the inhaler and running toward the driveway.

"Got it," he said, tossing the inhaler at his friend.

Xander took a puff of the albuterol, the humid mist coating the inside of his throat. It was an unpleasant feeling, but it calmed him down and opened his airways.

"We got trouble," Alison said. "We need to get in the van and head out."

Xander didn't listen. After putting the inhaler in his pocket, he used the bat as leverage to hoist himself up. He took a step toward the undead in the distance.

Sal slapped the hood down and hopped in the driver's seat. Alison poked out from the passenger door.

"Get. In. The van." Alison gritted her teeth.

With reluctance, Xander slid open the door and slammed it shut.

"All right, all right. Let's go to Fuckin' Freakz." Xander tossed the bat to the floorboard while Sal and Alison were buckling up. He sank into the back seat, making himself small.

Sal threw the shifter into reverse and floored the gas pedal, jolting Xander forward. Xander held onto Sal's seat to prevent himself from flying out the windshield. The wheels squealed. Sal slammed on the brakes and moved the shifter into drive. Xander, wide-eyed, scrambled for the seatbelt.

"Sorry, I haven't done this before." Sal had a big grin on his face. He drove away from the rising sun and the horde on their trail.

The town the kids had grown up in was left in oblivion. Alison winced when a woman, half dead and disemboweled, screamed for them to stop and help her. But Sal kept driving, and Alison looked the other way.

It wasn't just that woman. There were people all over the streets, fighting other humans and zombies. A group of men pulled a pregnant woman out of her car while her toddler screamed in the backseat. They took the car, even with the mother screaming and begging them to give her her baby. The men drove away with the stolen car and the toddler.

Xander watched the mother in the rearview mirror, being pulled back by a pair of undead. They chewed on her arms and shoulder, but the mom was in tears, trying to chase after the car, not caring about the monsters ripping at her flesh.

It didn't take long for the large sign of Fit Freakz to come into view—a recent construction from last summer. The building, all the landscaping, and the equipment inside was new, but it was apparent destruction had aged it.

There was a vegan restaurant next door called Lettuce Serve You, as well as a bougie coffee place on the other end. What was usually the nicest area had now become an abandoned ghost town, like it had been desolate for years.

Cars were piled on top of each other at the entrance and exit. Doors were open, with bodies toppling out. People were on the ground, with tire marks across their backs. And of course, the undead circled like vultures.

Sal pulled the van to a stop at the edge of the parking lot, surveying the scene. He left it in idle, in case they needed to peel out.

The undead shuffled aimlessly between the cars, their heads snapping toward any noise. The lot was already picked over and void of any human life. But the zombies avoided the dead bodies on the street. They must have been past their expiration date, even for those monsters baking in the summer sun.

"What do you guys think?" asked Alison.

"We can take them," Xander said.

"Only if we're not stupid about it." Sal turned around to look at Xander. "You were wild back at my place. We can't be making a scene. One at a time. No one gets left behind."

"We draw them out, one by one," said Alison. "It's a big lot, but there's only a handful I can see outside."

"We don't know if there are more hiding inside cars or elsewhere," noted Xander. "For all we know, an army of undead gym bros are lining the doors, waiting for losers like us to fuck around and find out."

"You know, Sal, it would be a good opportunity to get some bow practice in," said Alison.

"But I'm the getaway driver."

Sal smacked the wheel and made a *duh* motion with his hands.

"Switch me." Alison was maneuvering to trade places with Sal.

He blushed, with Alison practically in his lap. Sal slid out of her way and into the passenger seat. Xander grabbed the bow from next to him, along with the arrows, and handed them to Sal. The bloody garage tools and the bat were also brought with them. Alison hugged the pistol close to her.

The arrows were limited. Sal's dad had only bought two sets of twelve, so Sal was worried he would miss and not be able to recover them. Alison rolled down the passenger window halfway.

"Go on."

Sal pivoted and steadied the bow over the glass, loading the first arrow. This was the longest distance he had shot from. The last few times he had tried, his targets were only a few feet away.

"Pull up a little closer," said Sal. "To that one over there."

Alison rolled the car forward slightly. "That's as close as we're getting for now. I need enough space in case we need to bolt out of here. I won't be trapped."

Sal's arms shook when he tried to take aim. He had one eye open, focused above the arrow, attempting to align it with the zombie's head. But every time he had perfect sight, the zombie moved. Right as Sal was about to release the arrow, there were gunshots.

***

They had come from Lettuce Serve You.

Another group of three stepped into view. A rugged man who looked to be in his early forties was shooting zombies with precision. He had two women with him. One looked to be similar in age, smacking the undead with brass knuckles, a cigarette hanging from her lips.

The other Alison recognized as the girl she had crushed on at the gym.

She was tall and built in a way which made Alison's eyes wander. Brown coils were drenched in sweat and bouncing along her face. She ripped a battery-powered Sawzall straight down the head of a zombie.

Alison's cheeks became hot, and for the first time since the nightmare began, she had a goofy smile on her face.

A few undead went after the group, but they took them out with ease. The zombies from the Fit Freakz parking lot ran toward the gunfire, but the man didn't waste any bullets. He seemed so relaxed, like he did this every day. One by one, he shot them between the eyes.

"Great. People," Sal said. "After seeing what we did on the way here, I don't want to mess with them."

"Sal, we're just kids. And that guy is badass. Maybe they'd group with us if we show them we're not useless." Alison lit up, pushing herself out of the car and sliding open the back door to grab the crowbar. "Well, let's not let them have all the fun."

She ran up behind an undead—a heavyset man waddling toward the line of buildings—and bashed him with the crowbar with a solid whack. This caught the attention of her crush.

The girl smiled at Alison, kicking a corpse off herself she had just flayed open. She said something unintelligible to her friends. Alison couldn't read her lips, but the girl pointed at them.

Sal and Xander ran up behind, helping finish off the crowd of undead.

Alison grew cocky and ended up being surrounded by three, forcing her to take out her gun. She shot two bullets perfectly in the head of two of the zombies. The last one was impaled by the rusty metal of the crowbar—from the chin and out of the back of his head.

The man dropped his gun and kicked one of the corpses in front of him. Brass Knuckles Girl folded her arms and eyed the teens, saying something to the man. Gym Crush was fast approaching. She had light brown skin which held a moonlight glow, even in the sun's oppressive rays. Her lips looked soft, like cashmere.

"You kids all right?" she asked.

Alison's giddy smile molded into a frown.

"Yeah, we're good. You took all the fun from us," said Sal.

"Tough guys. I like that." Gym Crush pressed her tongue to her cheek and circled Alison first, then Sal and Xander.

Sal looked annoyed, and Xander seemed doing his best to try and look cool. He nodded to Brass Knuckle Girl, who approached him next.

"Sup."

"You're cute," she said. "Ain't he cute, Callum?"

She looked to the redheaded man, who hung back, watching his crew. Her teeth were yellow, but she appeared otherwise healthy. Brass Knuckles Girl had brown straggly hair and warm eyes.

Callum wasn't listening, but he responded anyway, in an almost catatonic state.

"Yap," he said.

"Oh, leave 'em alone, Toni. They look scared," Gym Crush said, putting the back of her hand on Sal's cheek.

"They ain't that young," replied Toni. "'Sides, I'm just playin'.'"

"Are you going to rob us?" Sal blurted.

"Why, you got anything good?" Callum sneered.

Sal snickered and Xander elbowed him.

"We got a few supplies, but we're looking to hang low in the gym for a bit. Our houses are…uh…not an option," said Sal.

"What a co-inky-dink," said Callum. "That's where we're headed. Seems we have a bit o' conflict of interest."

"Callum, you don't even know what that means." Gym Crush laughed.

"Shut your whore mouth, Jade." Callum puffed out his chest and swung himself at her. He meant to tower over her, but they were near the same height.

Jade was tall and fit, with a thick lower half. Callum was built, with a large upper half, a nonexistent backside, and scrawny legs.

Jade, Alison thought to herself. *Such a pretty name.*

Her face was as red as a cherry now, thinking sultry thoughts about that badass Jade with a Sawzall, defending her from monsters. Then her mind flashed to when Jade called her a kid, and she shook the thoughts from her head, wondering how old Jade actually was.

"Poor girl. I think she's mute," Jade said.

Alison's flush returned. She hadn't realized, with all the internal dialogue, she hadn't even greeted them.

"I'm Alison. Allie for short. And this is Xander, my brother, and Sal. Sal is…*was* our neighbor."

"Nice to meet you, Allie." Jade patted her on the back. "Why don't you three come with us? We could use a hand in this place. We can split whatever we find."

"Says you," Toni objected. "I ain't splitting shit." She held up a brass knuckle. "Right, Callum? We got here first."

Callum didn't agree with Toni. He instead joined the group to inspect the kids a little closer. The man reeked of tobacco and chemicals.

Alison reloaded her gun.

"All right, well, we're going in," she said.

"Long as I'm not babysitting, y'all can help," said Toni.

"Put the gun away. Bash'em and we'll cover you. I don't trust no kid with a gun." Callum took charge, herding the kids toward the entrance.

Toni took a final drag from her cigarette and tossed it on the ground.

Jade came up behind Alison. "Hey, do I know you from somewhere?"

"No."

"Huh. No, I swear I do," said Jade. "Oh well. Let's get on in here and kick some ass. I'm tired of fighting."

Callum stepped inside first, his rifle ready to sweep his surroundings.

"Stay close. And watch your corners."

Right as Callum said that, an undead grabbed Xander from around the corner. He snarled and clawed at Alison's brother. Trace amounts of blood pooled, but Xander had it taken care of.

They were in too tight of quarters for him to swing his bat without hurting the others, so Xander hit the zombie with the blunt end of the handle, knocking it backward. After creating distance from the group, he raised the bat above his head and did one final strike with a bit of a grunt.

Sal had his bow pointed to one that hadn't noticed the group yet. It was lapping up blood and intestines off the ground by the locker room entrance. Sal was steady this time, shoulder relaxed. The arrow launched, nearly missing, but impaled the back of its head.

"Nice shot, kid," said Callum.

"My name is Sal." A hint of annoyance was in his voice.

The gym was massive, with a large rounded help desk in the center. To the left was Freshies, the cafe Alison had talked about. Merchandise lined the wall on the right, with all types of clothing and swag displaying the Fit Freakz logo. There was also a cooler filled with energy drinks and homemade juices from the cafe.

Like a candy bar display at a store checkout, there were a bunch of high-protein snacks on shelving underneath the counter. Further back was the cardio equipment. Layered in were strength training machines, with dedicated rooms and classes in the far corner. Next were the water fill stations and the locker rooms.

Xander went up to the counter.

"Sweet…Snacks."

He extended an arm to grab a handful, and an undead popped up from behind the counter, grabbing him by the shirt. Xander was able to pull away, but there was another one back there too.

The zombies on the first day had looked human still. But these ones, even after just a day, had decomposed substantially. Their skin appeared rough, like construction paper. There was no life juice left in them. But they drooled along the counter and onto the treats, trying to crawl over rather than go around.

Toni came up behind Xander and held one of their necks on the counter, wailing on it with her brass knuckles. She was swift and moved onto the other one after two hits. That's all it took to crack open their heads like eggs.

Xander hadn't noticed the spikes before. They were gaudy and rhinestoned on the edges—not like the ones Xander had seen in video games. He gushed, admiring Toni's work.

"Bad. Ass," he said.

"Thanks. Cramping up a bit, though. Woof."

Toni smiled and momentarily removed the knuckles to shake her wrists.

"Switch up," said Callum. "We'll lead through."

With the immediate threat neutralized, the group spread out to secure the gym. Alison, Sal, and Xander stuck together. Jade and Callum took the lead, while Toni lagged behind, keeping an eye on their backs.

There were some picked-apart bodies on the ground by the cardio station. One woman had been eaten like a corn on the cob. She was plump, with big chunks taken out of her and a wound around her eye. Another woman's mouth had latched onto a treadmill. The handle went through her mouth and the back of her head. She dangled there, limp.

Near the cardio were sets of benches and lighter dumbbells facing a mirrored wall. The gang was looking rough. Not only were they dirty and bloody, but they didn't look much better than the corpses they were killing.

Alison frowned at her reflection, realizing how she must have appeared to Jade.

While she was checking herself out, a body sitting straight up on a bench startled her. It had a fifty-pound dumbbell, covered in bits of brain and guts, on its lap and one on the floor. Her eyes went to his face.

There wasn't one anymore.

"Looks like someone's been through here already," said Alison.

"No shit, Sherlock," Toni remarked.

"We should check the locker rooms first," suggested Jade. "Make sure nothing will come out of there and sneak up on us."

"It's too tight in there. We'll get gridlocked if we all go in there," said Sal.

"Then we make it easy," replied Callum. "Ladies go in the women's locker room, and men in the other. Damn. And *I'm* the dropout."

The locker room was just how Alison remembered. It was upper scale compared to the other gyms in the area. There was a huge, mirrored space for girls to dry their hair and do their makeup in the front, three different pods with lockers and benches, and bathroom stalls and sinks. In the back were the showers, sauna, and entrance to the pool. It still had the scent of the air fresheners the workers would stick above the lockers—a pleasant change from the smell of rotting corpses.

Jade put a finger to her lips and an arm out, blocking their path. She pointed at Alison and to the locker area, then to Toni and to the bathroom area. She mouthed, *And I'll check the showers.*

Beads of sweat dripped from Alison's forehead. Lockers were ajar, preventing her from scoping the pods fully. There was nowhere safe to put her back to, since the lockers formed a "U" shape. She rattled her nails on the cold metal to see if anything would stir. With trepidation, she walked down the row, using the barrel of her gun to close the open lockers.

Alison looked behind her.

Toni was stepping into the bathroom area like she was entering a cage match. Her fists were up and ready for action. There were five stalls. She nudged the first one open with her foot, ready to throw down, but there was nothing in there.

***

Jade quivered at the temperature changed. Steam permeated the air, making it humid. Through the stillness, the soft trickle of running water echoed. One of the showers was on at the end of the hall.

Jade held her weapon at an angle so she could, at any moment, swipe the blade up through someone's skull.

An awful stench lingered in the humidity. As much as Jade tried to keep quiet, the smell was just too terrible. She held her mouth in an attempt to mask her gagging. With some diligence, she swallowed it back down.

The small shower area was flooded. Brown-tinted water made a puddle about an inch thick.

Jade threw back the shower curtain, and her heart skipped a bit. She started up the Sawzall and was about the push down on the corpse like a Thanksgiving turkey, but it wasn't moving.

She turned off her weapon. Jade couldn't swallow it back this time. She leaned in and gagged all over the corpse.

The woman slumped against the shower wall had been cooked.

Scalding water crashed down onto her face, so hot it had peeled the woman's skin and tissue off, exposing her pearly white skull. Parts of her ear dangled, and she still had hair. But the majority of her breast bones and ribs were exposed, the water filling her cavity, bloating her. It looked like the corpse was about to pop.

Jade continued to gag, trying to turn off the faucet.

Then came a scream.

"Alison!"

The gruesome shower sight was soon forgotten. Jade rushed to Alison's aid, her boots sloshing against the puddles. She sprinted toward the lockers and started up the Sawzall. Toni was second to the scene, but Jade had already leaped into action.

Alison was on her back with one of those…*things*…snapping at her. She desperately tried to hold him back by the forehead with her left hand. His grimy claws pulled her hair toward his mouth, and he slurped it to get a taste of her. Alison's other arm reached for the pistol, which had fallen from her grip and skittered across the floor. Her fingertips were barely out of reach.

Jade didn't hesitate.

The Sawzall roared to life when she charged. She stood over the creature mounting Alison and ran the blade through the back of its head. The undead convulsed, its bile and remains squirting out of him. Jade kept going through the skull, until its cerebellum was halved. The blade was a hair away from Alison's face, stopping at the creature's nose.

Its head flayed open like a flower, and the remaining pieces of him fell. Jade retracted her weapon, crushing Alison beneath the gore.

The boys came rushing into the room at the sound of Alison's screams.

"Well, ain't that a sight," said Callum.

Xander and Sal hurried to Alison's side. They were speechless, ripping debris of human remains off her.

Alison was in shock, just lying there, still and unmoving.

Jade knelt next to her and tried to find her eyes, but Alison looked through her.

"Allie," she said. "It will be all right."

She extended a hand, but Alison left it untouched. Alison's lips quivered, and a single tear rolled down her cheek.

"Help me get her up," said Jade.

Xander and Jade put their palms under Alison's back and eased her to a sitting position. Once she was upright, Alison curled into a ball, holding her knees to her chest.

"You're safe now," Jade told her.

Xander pulled his sister to him. In this moment, he noticed the stench permeating his pits and staining his shirt.

"Sorry, I smell funky," he said. "Jade's right, though. You're safe now."

Toni put her hands on her hips. "A'ight, the party is over. Can we lock this shit down now?"

Callum rested his rifle on his shoulder and stretched. "Come on, Toni. We don't need their help."

He and Toni headed toward the sauna, scoping it out before shouting, "Clear!"

***

Callum hesitantly gripped the door to the pool, waiting for Toni's approval to open it. With caution, Callum pushed, putting the barrel of his gun through the crack before squeezing himself in and pressing his back to the wall. He slid to the side, giving Toni space to enter the room.

It was three on one, feasting on human remains and licking the bones clean. One more lingered in a corner, banging on a metal door to a closet, trying to claw its way in. Toni gave Callum a nod.

Attempting to not attract the attention of the three finishing their meal, the pair silently inched along the wall toward the rightmost pool area, closer to the supply closet. Callum rested his gun at his side, and his other hand fumbled the knife he had retrieved from his pocket.

But before Callum could sneak up on the creature, it sensed them. It whipped around, and a wildness flashed in its eyes before it pounced. It snarled and hissed.

Callum reacted just in time, plunging the blade straight through its forehead. The undead's jaw dropped, and its body slumped. Callum tore the knife from its skull and holstered it.

The clatter aroused the feasting group on the outer edges. Beady dead eyes locked on their new targets—Callum and Toni.

Callum got his gun ready to fire but hesitated on the trigger. Like dominoes, the zombies splashed into the pool. They struggled and thrashed but inevitably sunk to the bottom. In slow motion, they traveled to the edges, trying to get to their prey.

"We're good for now," said Toni. "Check that closet. Think there's fresh meat in there."

Callum rested his gun again, snickering at the trio of undead stuck in the bottom of the pool.

"Yep. I think you're right. Let's see what's behind door number one."

Callum gripped the handle, but it wouldn't turn. It wriggled when he shook it, like someone was holding tight on the other side. Callum released the handle and rubbed the stubble on his face in thought.

"I'm going to count to five," said Callum. "I'll back up and give you space. But if I get to five and you're still held up in there, I'll have to assume you're not friendly."

Callum paused for a moment and exchanged a glance with Toni, who was rolling her eyes. She rolled them so much, Callum was surprised they weren't stuck like that in the back of her head.

"One."

Silence.

"Two."

Silence.

"Now, I wouldn't even let my mama get past three." Callum reloaded his gun.

The sound of the empty clip falling to the ground must have scared whoever was behind the door. They spoke out.

"Wait! Wait! Don't shoot. Please, don't shoot."

Toni shoved Callum out of the way and opened the door.

A scrawny boy, no older than twenty, quivered with his arms raised. He was wearing a Fit Freakz uniform and a nametag reading: "Mohammed." His purple work shirt had been stained with body odor, and his dark hair curled and dripped with sweat. His facial hair struggled to take root on his face—straggling peach fuzz sprouting on his chin and upper lip.

Mohammed backed up and nearly tripped over the pool equipment. Foam water weights toppled onto him from the shelves above.

"Don't come any closer," he said. "I don't want to hurt you, but I will."

Toni and Callum shared a laugh. And when they started, they couldn't stop. Callum was red in the face, holding his gut, and Toni was near tears.

In a swift consecutive series of movements, Mohammed struck Callum three times, disarming him. Before Toni or Callum could react, he roundhouse kicked Toni, knocking her to the ground. Mohammed took this opportunity to run to the exit, with Callum's gun in tote.

"I'm sorry!"

"That ungrateful fuck!" said Toni. She sat on the ground, dumbfounded.

"No man in his right mind puts a hand on my woman!"

Callum's face was red with anger. He raised his knee and curb-stomped the freshly killed zombie's face. The impact of his boot against the skull popped its head open like a cracked egg. Blood and brain matter splattered all over Toni's breasts and face. The rest of its slimy yolk spread across the tile.

His hands closed into fists, and he sprinted after the boy.

CHAPTER 9

Mohammed ran through the locker room like a gust of wind. He was so quick, Jade, Alison, Sal, and Xander barely noticed when he brushed past.

"Hey, wait!" Sal shouted.

Mohammed didn't stop or turn around to acknowledge the group. When he blasted out of the locker room, he had to dart around the machines and gym equipment. At one point, he tripped over a barbell that had been left on the ground, but he quickly caught his footing.

Callum was right on his trail. If Mohammed had moved like the wind, Callum moved in like a storm. His footsteps thundered, and his boots clapped against the sleek floors.

"Callum!" Jade got up from comforting Alison, who seemed to snap out of her troubled state.

"What's going on?" she asked.

Toni moseyed up at this point. She ripped some paper towel from a nearby dispenser and patted the blood off her cheeks and breasts.

"That boy is a dead boy," she replied.

Callum didn't lose momentum. He closed in on Mohammed and grabbed him by the back of the shirt, just before Mohammed reached the door. With great force, Callum yanked him back, and Mohammed thwacked against a display of merchandise. The boy winced in pain, but he still held the gun close to his chest. Racks of leggings, hats, and water bottles crashed on his head.

Savoring the movement, Callum neared Mohammed. He cracked his knuckles and crinkled his face. "D-d-don't move."

With shaky hands, Mohammed raised the gun and pointed it at Callum.

"Callum, wait!" Jade had reached them at this point, with the others following behind her.

Callum looked down at the kid. His own gun pointed at him didn't seem to faze Callum. He took his meaty hands and grabbed the boy effortlessly, pinning him on the wall between two peg hooks. His breath was warm and sour, with a hint of dirt. The rifle sandwiched between them, Callum squeezed the boy's neck.

"I can take care of myself, Callum. I'm fine. Just shook up a little," Toni said.

She had her arms crossed and hips slumped to one side. Toni eyed the rack of items, took a Fit Freakz baseball cap, and fit it over her head.

Callum's veins popped from his temples, and his face grew an even deeper red. He wasn't hearing anyone at that moment.

"Now, I don't like to be ignored," Toni said.

She grabbed a stapler off the front desk and opened it up. With a solid grip, she whacked Callum in the back of the head, and the metal snapped against his skull like a whip.

Stunned, he released the boy and grabbed the pulsing area on his scalp.

Mohammed sighed with relief and ran for the door again, in hopes of slipping out.

"Fucking Christ," said Toni.

She threw the stapler like a boomerang, and it struck Mohammed in the head, knocking him out cold in his tracks.

***

Mohammed came to sitting on the ground, with those strangers who tried to kill him hovering around him. Across was Callum. He was gruff and burly, staring down Mohammed. But Callum was tied to a wall with large black ropes. Rope burn coated the pale freckled skin under his shoulders.

"Easy, big boy." Toni patted Callum on the head like a dog. "Now, we're going to play nice because I don't have the energy to deal with crypt-walkers *and* testosterone in one night. Capisce?"

When Callum didn't reply, Toni turned to Mohammed.

"I'm Toni. This is Jade, Xander, Sal, and Alison."

Mohammed made a move to get up and run again, but his body was stiff. He looked down, realizing he was tied up too. The cord of a weighted cable machine had been wrapped around him, cutting into his skin. Burning pain ignited when he struggled against the bindings.

"I recognize this kid," Jade said.

She had a mouthful of something. The others also picked at snacks, which appeared to have come from the front desk. Shiny wrappers were in a pile around the tied-up people. Jade added another to it.

"He's the floor buffer kid," said Alison.

Jade gave Alison a look. "You work out here?"

"Yeah, I do. Well...*did*," Alison replied.

"Hmm. Well, it makes sense why we're all here, then. It was smart of you guys to come here. Not most people's first choice. That's why it's perfect."

"Yeah, those poor people at Whole Foods down the road," said Xander. "It was a Katamari of humans, both dead and undead."

"A kata-what-y?" asked Alison.

"Don't be a fucking nerd," said Sal. "This isn't a video game. It's real life."

Xander scoffed at Sal.

Mohammed wriggled again—a futile attempt to break free.

"Easy, kid," said Toni. "Stay awhile. Want a bite?"

Toni held up a protein bar under Mohammed's nostrils. A bite had been taken out of it. The chocolate-coated thing had no scent, but nonetheless, his stomach growled, so he nodded.

"If you untie me, I'd love one," Mohammed said.

"Nah." Toni took back her offer and another bite of the snack. "Not happenin'."

"Untie me now, you cunt!" Callum gritted his teeth.

"Babe, you turn me on so hard when you're grumpy." She grabbed Callum by the chin and made a pouty face.

He ripped his head away. "This punk took my gun and knocked you on your ass. I defend your ass, and this is how I'm treated? Like a damn dog!"

Mohammed swallowed hard, trying to find his voice. His vocal cords rubbed against his larynx, and he croaked like a frog. Throat swollen and in pain from shouting, it came out a hoarse whisper.

"He's right. I'm a punk. I'm a punk, and I'm sorry. I'm just defenseless and alone. I want to survive."

Xander shook his head and walked over to Mohammed. "If I untie you, promise you won't try stealing our shit."

"Since when are you calling the shots?" Toni put her arm in front of the boy. "Trust isn't something you just give to thieves."

"I hate to say it, but I agree with the scary lady on this one," said Sal.

Xander rolled his eyes and started to unravel the cords holding the boy. Frantic, Mohammed tried to wiggle his way out as soon as they were loose.

Xander whispered under his breath, "Stop freaking out. Don't make me look stupid."

Mohammed's heart rate skyrocketed. But the fight-or-flight started to dissipate when no one stopped Xander. Even Callum slumped back against the wall and broke his death stare. Mohammed gulped and let out a sigh of relief.

"Thank you."

"No problem." Alison took a bottle of water and offered it to him.

He immediately snatched it up and chugged the entire thing.

"How long were you in that closet?" asked Jade.

"Overnight, I think. I don't know. At least one night. It's hard to tell when you're crouched in a ball, doing nothing for hours, while your friends and coworkers eat each other inches away from you."

Tears welled up in Mohammed's eyes when he recalled the events. The screams of terror his friends had made rang in the back of his mind, haunting him. He had been barricaded within the supply closet with his fear, while the people around him suffered. Lost in thought, he didn't hear Sal speak out.

"Hello?"

"Oh, what? Sorry. I spaced out."

"I asked you if you thought anyone else was here? Any other places we should check?"

The people Mohammed had lost flashed through his head like a Rolodex. He tried to recall who had been working that day and who didn't escape in time. He wasn't sure since he had been locked up, but he responded.

"It's just me. The rest of them…Well, you saw them."

The weight of Mohammed's words hung heavily in the air. Each of the survivors seemed to process their grim reality: once vibrant and living people had been reduced to the ravenous undead.

"What about family?" asked Xander. "Your folks are probably looking for you."

He shook his head and didn't respond.

"You don't know," said Alison. "You haven't been out there. You should at least check if they—"

"They disowned me," said Mohammed. "My roommate, Chaz, he's all I got." Mohammed's eyes went wide, and he was lost in thought again. Then his face drooped. "All I *had*."

Xander worked on untying Callum. He didn't get up or pounce when the ropes fell to the ground. Callum just stretched and kept close eyes on the new kid.

"Thanks," he muttered. "Jade. Toni. We've had enough playtime. I didn't sign up to babysit. Let's get moving."

"Oh, come on. It's perfect here. We got food, water, showers…" Jade paused, turning slightly green. "Anyway, it's stupid to wander aimlessly. It's best to stay put and wait shit out a bit. Maybe this will all end soon."

Callum laughed and wheezed. Black tar definitely coated his lungs from years of smoking.

"Ain't no one getting out of this mess anytime soon," he said.

"What makes you so sure?" asked Sal.

"Y'all didn't see downtown, did ya?" Callum snickered. "'Course you didn't."

"What's downtown?" Xander pressed.

"There's more of those fuckers than there are of us, that's for sure. It's a swarm down there."

"I agree with Jade that we should stay here a while," offered Alison. "If what Callum says is true, I don't want to go find out. That just solidifies that this place is fine for now. Like I told you all it would be."

She glared at Xander and Sal. They hung their heads low.

Mohammed looked around, taking in his surroundings in full. The place he had worked at was in complete disarray. Bodies hung from equipment, impaled, and blood was everywhere. He recognized one of his regulars on the ground. The man had been a gentle giant, but no one ever talked to him or messed with him. He talked to Mohammed, though. Every morning, except Sundays, the man would show up at six and tell him good morning by name, even though Mohammed had never asked for his.

Mohammed stared at the lump of muscled flesh a few feet away, feeling guilty he had never gotten his name.

"Nice to meet you all," Mo said. "I'm sorry about earlier. Really."

Toni put her arm around him and pulled him close, like a giant, ginger teddy bear.

"That taekwondo shit was pretty impressive. I ain't mad 'bout it," she said.

"How'd you know that's what it was?" A half-smile crept up Mo's face.

"That ninja shit you were doing? That's what that was?" asked Callum.

Mo was relieved Callum's aggression had simmered. He much preferred annoyance and slight bullying—the type of social interactions he was used to, anyway. It made things feel normal.

"Ninjas are Japanese culture," he said. "Taekwondo is Korean."

"Only Japs are ninjas? Well, I'll be damned," said Callum.

Sal rolled his eyes. "Oh, you're one of *those* guys."

He was obviously referring to Callum and his prejudiced comment, but Callum didn't catch on.

"See? Brown kid gets it." Callum pointed at Sal. "Goddamn, we have the whole Reading Rainbow up in here."

Sal couldn't help but laugh. "Some shit never changes," he whispered.

Then he stood up and made an announcement.

"We didn't find an office area or breakroom. This place isn't secured yet." He looked to Mo and took out his bow. "Show me where it is."

"We have a few to take care of still at the pool," Toni chimed in. "I'll grab the floaties."

The group dispersed, and Mo lead Sal to the office area. He moved slowly, checking his surroundings with paranoia.

"Keep moving," Sal demanded. "What's the problem?"

"Lay off," Mo said. "How are you so calm and collected?"

"I'm not."

"Sure seems like it."

"How old are you, anyway?"

"Sixteen. You?"

"Fifteen. You go to Maple High too?"

"No."

"Belford?"

"No."

"I give up," said Sal.

"I dropped out."

“Oh.”

The boys reached an office door.

“Here it is. Have fun.” Mo crossed his arms and stepped back.

“Don’t be a baby. You’re coming with me.”

“The fuck I am. I don’t have a weapon.”

Someone overheard their arguing. The growling and hissing of a zombie on the other side of the door startled them.

“I’ll stand back, and you get the door. I’ll shoot ’em,” Sal said.

“No way, man. Give me a weapon.”

“What do I look like, an arms dealer? Grab literally anything here. I need some shooting practice.”

There was a nearby rack of kettle balls. Mo grabbed a ten-pound weight by the handle. The zombie on the other side banged on the door, desperate to get to them.

“Ready?” Mo asked.

“Hang on.”

Sal readied his bow and loaded the arrow. He tried his best to line up where he imagined the target’s head would be when Mo opened the door.

“Ready.”

Mo gripped the kettle ball tightly in his right hand and swung the door open with his left, using it as a shield and taking cover. Out tumbled his boss, Darrel.

Darrel had been a stereotypical gym bro who used steroids and creatine like crack. Mo was also pretty sure he did cocaine. Darrel came barreling out like a football player, ready to tackle Sal.

Sal released the arrow, and it flew past Darrel’s head.

“Shit!”

Sal backed up and fumbled to load another. He was able to get a second arrow off quickly, but he didn't pull back with enough force. The arrow jumped from Sal's hands and bounced off the big man's chest.

"Do something!"

Mo came up behind his boss, swinging the weighted ball into the back of his head. It made the zombie flinch, but it didn't bring him down. Darrel was tough, even as a dead guy.

Without the element of surprise, Mo couldn't get close enough to get in another swing. He fell back, trying to increase the distance between them. But while looking over his shoulder at Darrel, Mo slipped on a puddle of blood and caught himself on a machine.

Darrel grabbed Mo, drool dripping onto his face. The zombie's skin was gray and had small craters. Dried blood covered his chest and biceps. But that wasn't what creeped out Mo the most.

Instead of focusing on the fact he was probably going to die, that his boss would rip him apart and kill him, Mo focused on the smile Darrel had on his face. Somewhere in the carcass wanting to eat him was his bully of a boss, finally about to terminate him.

Just in time, Sal saved the day.

He shot off an arrow, and it went through Darrel's head.

Mo was hyperventilating and didn't move from his awkward position when Darrel tumbled to the floor. Sal retrieved his arrows, not saying anything. He cleaned them off with his shirt and put them back in the quiver over his shoulder. Then, he set about looting the office.

Mo followed quietly behind, watching Sal ransack the small room. Every single desk drawer had been ripped open. He found shooters of whiskey, which he tossed on top. Mostly everything in there was garbage and paperwork.

"What a waste," said Sal.

"What were you expecting?"

"I don't know. Something. *Anything* for risking my life, I guess."

"Were you expecting to find heavy artillery? We're in a gym, for fuck's sake."

"The only guns I need are right here." Sal patted his bicep.

Mo tried not to, but he laughed.

"I'm sorry. I'm sorry. But that's too funny."

Sal shrugged Mo in the shoulder. "Fuck off."

When Mo barely felt the punch, he laughed harder.

"Okay, okay. I'll fuck right off."

Mo watched Sal walk away, while he lingered in the office. When Sal had left his eyesight, Mo decided to take a deeper look.

First, he got the satisfaction of kicking his former boss in the face. But when that didn't satisfy him, Mo felt grossed out. He took a sweat rag from Darrel's gym bag and placed it over the zombie's face.

CHAPTER 10

Six months earlier, Evelyn had been told she had less than a year to live. Two months earlier, she had been told she probably wouldn't make it to Christmas.

The doctors at St. Henry's Hospital were her friends, mostly. So when Harvey thumbed through her CAT scans with that look on his face, it irritated Evelyn.

"Give it to me straight, Harvey. Am I dying?"

Harvey rested his elbow on his desk, palm on his cheek, and sighed.

"Ev, you're here now, aren't you? We all die a little more every day. C'est la vie. What is life without death? Hell, nearly seventy billion cells die each day in the human body, and it can replenish up to eighty million more before the Earth turns full circle. I think that's—"

"Harvey! Cut the bullshit. How long?"

Dr. Harvey let out another sigh and bit the tip of his pencil. Bite marks circled around the top, by the eraser.

"I think you should make plans to stay inpatient, Ev."

"I'm not rotting in this place. No way. I'll be with my family."

"Maybe you should talk to Aaron about this. I'm sure he would want you in a place that you could be monitored. A place that could help extend your life."

Evelyn went quiet. She leaned back in the blue leather chair and crossed her arms, breaking eye contact with Harvey.

"Oh, Ev…" Harvey sat up and scooted toward Evelyn, throwing the files on his desk. "Ev, please tell me you told him."

Evelyn shook her head.

"And the kids? They don't know either?"

Evelyn hid behind her blond curtain bangs and silently cried. She gripped the loose folds in her pants on her lap, a reminder of her recent, uncontrollable weight loss. Silent and ashamed, she sobbed.

Lost in thoughts of death and leaving her family behind, she let Harvey comfort her. She fell into his chest, the tears and snot running all over his white coat. Evelyn wanted to apologize and reject the comfort, but she didn't have the strength too. He rubbed her back.

Evelyn could feel his wedding rings through the silk of her shirt as much as she felt the eyes of the other nurses through the slits of the blinds in Harvey's office.

"It'll be okay, Ev," he said. "We're going to get you through this."

"How are you going to get me through a stage three astrocytoma, Harvey?"

Evelyn tugged on Harvey's snot-drenched coat to pull herself up. Her glassy eyes made contact with his, and he looked away. There it was. That look again.

"Harvey…What is it? Did it mutate?"

"Glioblastoma."

Harvey rolled to his desk and grabbed the files, stacking them neatly back together. He handed them to Evelyn.

"That's what it is now. It moved from your medulla oblongata, left a mess of your cerebellum, and metastasized a large portion of the right cerebral hemisphere. To be honest, I'm surprised you're not keeled over already."

Evelyn flipped through the scans and notes. She knew all the medical terminology, but Harvey's words and the diagnosis on the papers blurred together into a spiral floating off the pages. Her head pulsed on queue with her daily 2:00 p.m. migraines. Evelyn stared at the scan of the golf-ball-sized tumor in the right half of her brain, and it throbbed in real time. It was as if Satan himself had a hold on her, his claws digging into her head, like Hell's personal stress ball.

She couldn't take it anymore. With a sense of calm and control, she swallowed her tears and gave the files back to Harvey. Everything in the room and around them became very loud. The lights were so bright, she heard them like sirens. Evelyn took a deep breath in and let it out until the ringing in her ears stopped.

"But with radiation and chemo," Harvey continued, "there's a chance you could make it."

"Less than five-percent chance," said Evelyn.

Her voice was sullen. She stared out the slits of the blinds, at her coworkers running from room to room, station to station. The sick kept getting sicker and the nurses' feet even quicker, but the sick always outnumbered them. Evelyn was just a number now, a statistic, less than human.

"I wouldn't say you're that far off…" Harvey paused.

He took a moment to rifle through his desk drawers. Harvey pushed around his hoard of papers and referrals. In the mix was a brochure.

Unlike the rest on the display stands in the waiting room, this one was different. It was simple and white, with thin turquoise letters that read: "Vera." Harvey handed the pamphlet to Evelyn. She begrudgingly accepted it.

"It's a new clinical trial. Just another one of those things that might buy you more time. You know the drug companies give us the same product with a different label every month these days. But…I don't know. This one seems different."

Evelyn opened the pamphlet, and the inside was just as bare as the outside.

There was a *before* side and an *after* side. The *before* side on the left had a child's drawing of a house. A stick figure stood outside with a frown. Little faces in the window on the inside of the house also had frowns. The *after* side was an artist's rendition of the house on the left. It had deep green brushstrokes for the siding with streaks of sunlight on the panels. A family sat inside at the dinner table, smiles on their faces. At the bottom it said: "After life, doesn't have to be afterlife," with a phone number and email address.

"This is…"

"Weird," Harvey finished her thought. "Yes, I thought so too."

"Thanks, I guess…" Evelyn picked up her purse from the ground and shoved the brochure inside of it. "I'll keep this in mind."

"Maybe something to discuss with Aaron and the kids."

"Aaron can suck a dick."

Harvey's eyes widened. "Woah. Uh. I…"

"Sorry." Evelyn slumped and clutched her purse to her stomach. "I've been on edge lately about that. It's a touchy subject."

"Uhm, noted," said Harvey. "Well. If you ever need anyone to talk to, feel free to stop by my office."

Evelyn got up from the chair. Harvey stood up to send her off.

"Pretty sad if I need to seek therapy from my coworkers. I'll see you on third shift later," said Evelyn. "I heard you're working doubles."

"Ev, why don't you take a step back from work? We got things handled here. Janet offered to take on more shifts. We have those interns looking to dive in too."

"Are you firing me?" Evelyn scoffed.

"Fire you? Goodness, no. It's just a suggestion. Think about it, Ev."

"Yeah, I will."

Evelyn rolled her eyes the moment she turned from Harvey and strolled through the door. She stopped in the doorframe and pressed her tongue to her cheek.

"You know, Harvey. I'm not dead yet."

The ladies at the desk quickly rummaged through papers and started clicking randomly on their mice and clacking keyboards. One of them side-eyed Evelyn.

"Shut up, Janet." Evelyn stopped and confronted her.

"But…But I didn't say anything."

"You didn't have to. I can see it all over your face. You nosy, mean-girl bitches."

Janet gasped, and the other women snickered behind their paperwork.

Evelyn didn't give time for a further reaction. She stabbed the elevator button until the doors opened.

Harvey shook his head at her through the blinds while Evelyn stood inside the elevator, jabbing the button to go downstairs.

***

When she got home, Xander was holed up in his room, playing video games. She didn't know the names of any of them, but this one involved shooting zombies and something to do with the military. He often shouted through his headset. The noise made her head throb, so she went to his bedroom and closed his door.

Alison was out with friends and wouldn't be back until later.

Evelyn never knew anymore with her. It irritated her endlessly. All Evelyn wanted was a courtesy text so she knew how many plates to set for dinner. But all she got back was "IDK" if she received any text at all. Evelyn tossed her phone on the counter and opened the fridge.

She didn't even bother messaging Aaron, knowing he would just say he was working late again. The nerve of him. That was the oldest excuse in the book. Evelyn would much rather he say he was banging the receptionist than tell her another fib about a late customer teams meeting.

Evelyn moved around leftovers, expired milk, and wilted spinach, wondering what to make. Instead, she leaned over to the cupboard to the right of the fridge and pulled out a wine glass. She rubbed the dust off the rim with her shirt and put the glass under the spout of box wine in the fridge.

The luscious, translucent-pink nectar swirled in her glass. She let it fill to the brim before she swigged the wine in its entirety.

Then Alison barged through the door.

"Hi, Mom," she said. "What's for dinner? I'm starving."

Of course, she was.

***

All these memories flooded into Evelyn's mind when she stood in front of her former workplace, St. Henry's Hospital. In a matter of two days, it had been destroyed.

Windows were blown out. Glass and dead bodies coated the sidewalks and the emergency room drop-off. Cars clustered in every direction, trapping ambulances in a circle of abandoned vehicles. Small fires lit up the area.

Evelyn's snarling minion scoped out the scene for anyone left alive—anyone left they could eat.

In the mess of cars, there was a torso smashed between the hood of a Bronco and the bumper of a BMW. It was a man gushing blood and shaking violently, but he was still alive. His face was torn and battered.

Evelyn barely recognized Harvey.

His white coat was now crimson. His flashy engraved wedding band gave it away. That and the stupid look he always had on his face. He looked up at her with relief and then mercy.

"P-p-please. K-kill me."

Fred shambled toward Harvey and took in his scent. His head was still limp from the severed bone and spinal cord.

Harvey's near-death state was intoxicating. Evelyn felt it. So did Fred. As delicious as her former boss looked, pity balled in her stomach. Somewhere so deep below the surface, Evelyn still had feelings for Harvey. She wanted to eat him but couldn't.

But still, he begged her to. He begged her to take his life.

"P-p-Pl—"

Blood gurgled in his throat. Harvey was choking on his own fluids.

Fred growled deeply, a smile curling on his face. He reached out and caressed Harvey's cheek. His eyes bulged from his head, and his long tongue coiled outside his lips. His focus found Evelyn, asking her for permission.

And she gave it to him.

Fred leaped at Harvey like a jumping spider, grabbing onto his shoulders for support. He ate Harvey face-first. Harvey's intestines started to rip from between the two vehicles, the bowels leaking onto the ground like candy from a piñata.

Pieces of Harvey splattered onto Evelyn. She couldn't let him go to waste, so she licked her lips. Fred finished quickly. He was bloated, shoving piles of sludge and tattered meat into his mouth. Evelyn approached, and he instantly dropped the flesh and wiped his face.

The golden wedding band shone brightly on Harvey's finger still. It was a stark contrast to the speckled gray of her vision. His arm had been torn from its socket, most of the meat picked away from it. It was palm up on the pavement, waving to her. She crouched and caressed what was left of the arm and held the hand. Evelyn wanted to cry, but no tears left her eyes. So instead, she slid the band off of his finger and pocketed the memento.

Evelyn pushed her thoughts to Fred—he seemed to understand this way. She couldn't hear his, but she could feel them. He was willing to follow her, to listen to her. She told him to come, and he came. They limped side by side, around the maze of bodies and cars, to the entrance of St. Henry's Hospital.

CHAPTER 11

Back in the squatting area at the gym, Alison and Xander sat back-to-back. They stayed alert, vigilant to the next attack. Jade wandered, picking up pieces of trash in the immediate area.

"So, this place is great and all…" Jade picked up body parts too mangled to be identified and tossed them into a nearby trash can. "But what are we going to do with all the dead bodies? I get a feeling this is even too much for a Hefty bag."

Alison broke her concentration on watch duty at Jade's comment. She looked at the place. *Really* looked at it now. She had been so focused on killing and surviving, she really hadn't been squeamish about the corpses decorating the floor. But now they had a smidge of security, Alison's stomach turned.

"We could drag them outside," she suggested.

"We don't have long before nightfall," said Xander. "I don't want to cause attention to us here. I just want to sleep tonight. I'm…I'm so tired."

He slumped back.

"You're saying you're good sleeping next to…*that*?"

Jade pointed to a fifty-pound barbell plate that had been smashed into someone's face a few feet away from where they planned to sleep. The weight had severed the head from the spinal cord.

Xander couldn't look at it past its feet. He couldn't think too hard about the body being real, not some Halloween decoration. Not a video game. Not a father. Or a son. Or a brother. No. He couldn't start down that rabbit hole. Xander quivered and looked away.

"Okay. I see your point," he said. "But these meatheads are all jacked. How the hell are we going to get them out of here."

"I have an idea." Alison smirked and bounced to her feet. "Be right back."

"Don't say that!" Xander yelled. "Jeez, you really should watch more movies."

Jade laughed.

Alison returned with a large black metal cart. Its wheel squeaked like a broken shopping buggy.

"Oh, why didn't I think of that!" Jade exclaimed. "This is perfect!"

"Where the hell did you get a shopping cart? That looks like it came from Home Depot," said Xander.

"It's a power sled," replied Jade. "Help me get this guy onto it. Let's test it out," she said to Xander. "Alison, can you hold it steady?"

Alison nodded. "Yep. I got it. Here. I'll bring it closer."

Jade had a surprising amount of strength. Lumps on her biceps bulged when she heaved the corpse onto the sled. Two vertical poles impaled the corpse.

"Fuck, didn't think it would do that," said Alison.

She helped Jade pick the sliding body off the poles and wedge him in between. Xander struggled with the lower half. It dangled off the end of the cart, which was fine. It wasn't big enough to hold the entire body. The corpse would fit much better horizontally.

"One a time, back and forth, will take forever," said Xander.

"Fuck that. I've been training." Jade heaved the sled forward to another corpse.

This one was the one lodged onto the equipment, like a stake through her. Jade yanked her off and tossed the body onto the other corpse.

"And I can tell you've been training too," Jade said to Alison. "What for?"

"I do mostly running. I did track at my high school. It's stupid, I know. Childish."

"No, it's not. I did wrestling in high school. But that was a few years ago. Only girl on the team and no one took me seriously. But I kicked ass, and all the boys were too scared to put their hands on me. It was great."

"*Great…*" Xander muttered under his breath. He moved onto the limbs and chunks of organs on the floor, slopping pieces of intestine in a garbage can.

"That's bad ass!" said Alison. "Do you still do it?"

"I'm going to take out this trash," said Xander.

But neither girl paid attention to him, just continued hoisting corpses on the sled. They didn't need him. So, Xander heaved a full bag over his shoulder and headed for the back door by the pool.

***

"Girl, I'm pro. Callum was my personal trainer," said Jade. "He's retired now. I'm sure you were wondering why we were together. Make a pretty odd trio."

"Yeah, but I wasn't going to comment," replied Alison. "Those other two are definitely a good match. Seemed like you were third-wheeling them a bit."

They heaved a corpse together now, swinging it back and forth for momentum, tossing it onto the full sled.

"Yeah, would be nice to have a fourth wheel."

Alison blushed.

"Not…that I was implying anything," Jade said. "Just joking."

"Yeah, I know."

"Well, cart's full. We should take it out back."

Jade mustered all her strength to push the sled, but it barely shifted a few inches. Her muscles bulged, and blood vessels became visible on her face.

"Need help?"

"No, I got it."

Jade built up power, and once the wheels started going, her pace picked up. It was still a snail's speed, but it was something. Alison dawdled beside her.

"Fine, but I get a turn once you reach the cable weights," she said.

***

Xander pushed open the door to the pool, where the back entry was. He passed Callum and Toni making out on the tile by bloated corpses. He was ripping at her tank top and mixing sweat with hers.

Xander cleared his throat when he passed. They didn't take a hint and stop.

Sunlight leaked in the gym after Xander opened the door, but the calming warmth didn't last. A group of people in the near distance had been swarmed by a large crowd of undead. Xander tossed the bag as far as he could away from the building and watched the attack unfold.

The people were already good as dead, and the zombies kept coming, flocking to the group like moths to a flame. Harsh rays of the setting sun beat down on Xander. He left the back door ajar.

To the left was the back alley of the vegan restaurant. A semi had been abandoned by a dock, its lift gate up. Xander was curious but didn't want to be outside without a weapon. His bat was in the middle of the gym by the snacks. He looked around at his options and checked by the dumpster behind the gym.

Xander sifted through junk. It was mostly just garbage—to be expected. There was a mountain of plastic water bottles and wipes. Underneath the desert of trash was some discarded workout equipment. Then Xander saw the perfect weapon.

Someone had thrown out a perfectly good hammer. It was lodged underneath a heavy set of weight plates. Xander tried to pull it out, but it wouldn't budge. He was half in the garbage pit now, trying to leverage his foot against the bin.

Then the trash moved in waves.

Something was in the dumpster with him. Xander froze when two beady black eyes stared at him through the pile of waste.

The beast lurched forward and clawed at Xander.

He hopped back and shouted, "Help! I've been bit!"

But he spoke too soon.

It was only a raccoon darting out of the receptacle, clawing at Xander to push himself up and away from him. Then it ran off into the shadows.

Xander's heart fluttered out of his chest. He gripped it and focused on his breathing. Blood trailed down his forearm from the claw marks.

When Xander turned around, he was greeted by a zombie. It got ahold of him when he screamed. With no weapon to fend it off, Xander was helpless. Yelling was his only option. He was terrified when he saw more of them round the corner.

And he had left the door open.

"Alison!"

She was in danger, and he had put her in it. Xander did his best to squeeze tightly onto the zombie's wrists, keeping a foot on its chest to keep it away. But this one was bigger than him. And determined.

Xander was backed up against the dumpster now. His legs felt like jelly. It had only been seconds, but he couldn't hold much longer.

Just in time, Callum came rushing through the door, fully nude and dick out, erect, gun blazing.

"Lean back, now!" Callum shouted.

Xander did as he was told.

Callum took his shot and domed the zombie. Ringing blasted through Xander's eardrums while Callum finished off the rest coming toward the door. The zombie fell forward on him.

The pain in his ears didn't hurt as much as his arm, though. With little strength, Xander pushed the corpse off of him and inspected the fresh bite wounds on his wrist.

Xander's vision blurred. He stared at the bite marks. They swirled into the shape of an Ouroboros symbol—two snakes eating each other. His heart throbbed, and a cold sweat broke across his forehead. He stumbled backward, clutching his wrist.

Finally, his knees buckled, and he fell forward onto the corpse that had bitten him. Heat swam through his veins. His pulse felt like fire.

Callum, still standing nude and holding his smoking gun, glanced at Xander and cursed under his breath. Toni sauntered out casually, snapping her bra back together. She shook her head at Callum, and he reloaded his gun.

***

Jade and Alison were almost to the pool lobby when they heard screams and gunshots. They quickly abandoned the power sled and rushed outside. Sal and Mo followed behind them.

"Whelp. Sorry 'bout your brother." Callum lined Xander in his sights.

Alison jumped on him, disregarding everything else.

This tactic didn't disarm Callum. He barely stumbled. It just made his member stand taller. He sighed while Alison yelled at him and beat on his head.

"It's the only way," Toni said. "We don't have much time."

***

Xander shook, looking around at his sister, his friend, and those strangers. They wanted him dead. But Xander was afraid to die. He didn't want to put anyone in danger, but he refused to be put down. So, he pleaded for his life.

Sal rushed to his friend's aid.

"There's gotta be a first aid kit in there. Mo! Go inside and find it. You should know where it is."

Mo nodded and ran back inside.

"That won't help," Jade said. "I'm sorry, kids, but I've seen one too many people turn."

"Get her off of me before a shoot her too." Callum looked at Sal with dead eyes.

Jade intervened and tore Alison away from Callum. She coached her through the situation, telling her to be there for her brother. This worked. Alison ran to Xander and collapsed in front of him. She took his arm to look at the bite marks. Afraid to touch them, she cried, her hand hovering over his.

Xander was shaking now.

"Move," Callum said. He knelt by Xander and repeated himself when nobody obeyed. Callum whipped out his pocketknife and shook his head. "This gonna hurt like a bitch."

"What are you doing?" Sal asked, but they all knew what was happening.

Alison was stunned but didn't move. Callum ripped Xander's hand toward him and steadied it on his knee.

"No, no no!" Xander snapped out of his fugue. "You can't!" he yelled.

But he did.

Because the blade was so small, Callum had to dig deep before carving around the wrist. He sliced into Xander and moved the knife around in a circle, like skinning an avocado. It was sharp enough to get the job done. It just took longer than Xander could stand. He wasn't screaming long before he passed out from the pain.

***

Callum hacked away, his face grim and focused. Blood spurted out in rhythmic pulses, splattering on Callum's bare chest. Alison winced, turning her head away, but she didn't leave. She couldn't abandon Xander now, not when he needed her the most.

Sal hovered close by but had backed away when Callum started sawing. His eyes were wide, a mixture of horror and helplessness.

"I'll go grab a shirt or something. Stop the bleeding." Sal ran inside the gym.

Toni watched with detached interest, as if the scene before her were nothing more than a slasher flick. Jade stood ready, her eyes scanning their surroundings for any approaching threats.

A flock hovered in the distance. The noise had pulled them toward the gym.

"Guys," Jade said. "We have problems. Like, plural."

Mo hurried over, panting, first aid kit in hand. He held it up and dropped it when he noticed Callum sawing through the bone. "Praise, Allah."

Mo backed away, shielding his vision from the grotesque sight.

Xander's wrist hung limp and barely detached. With ease, Callum sliced through the final flap of skin and tissue, and it dropped to the ground. Blood gushed out fast. He had already lost so much. It wouldn't be too long before he died from blood loss.

Sal ran back at lightning speed and almost couldn't stop. He dropped to Xander with a handful of Fit Freakz shirts and wrapped one of them around his friend's severed stump.

Callum used one of the shirts to clean his knife and put it back in his pocket. He stood up.

"Well. I did the hard part. You all figure out the rest."

"He needs a doctor!" Alison yelled.

"Guys!" Jade interjected. "I *said*, we have a problem. "Look!"

She pointed to the setting sun in the distance and the horde of zombies coming their way.

Chaos ensued while the group grabbed whatever they could fit in their bags and arms in one trip. Alison and Sal struggled to carry Xander, his arms over their shoulders. Callum ripped a pair of sweatpants off the display rack and stumbled to get his feet in them. He threw his gun over his shoulder and located his knife.

"Move."

Callum relieved Sal and Alison of Xander. He lifted the boy with ease and ran out the door.

The team worked in silence, filling up the minivan with the possessions they thought to bring. Xander was tossed like the gym bags into the back seat. Alison shoved everyone out of the way to buckle him in.

Leaders of the horde were already pushing through toward the front of the gym. But it was evident something was off about them.

Their faces were contorted and melting off their skulls. Flames burned from beneath their blackened skin, licking the hollows of their ribs like ebbing candles. Walking fire swarmed the space.

"Let's go!" Mo yelled.

It was a tight squeeze in the van. Three had become seven in less than a day's time. Toni took the wheel and turned the keys in the ignition. The Dodge Caravan hummed to life but sputtered in between the engine's roar.

Toni threw the shifter in reverse and floored the pedal. She backed up into one of the flaming zombies. Blunt force clashed into the back bumper, but the minivan didn't take any damage. A bit of blood and charred remains splattered on the rear window, so Toni turned on the back wiper. It only smeared the blood into a brown ooze.

"Hand me a cigarette, will ya, babe?"

Toni held her hand out behind her while she wove through the debris, stopped cars, and corpses on the road.

"Uhhh…" Callum patted down his pants. "Don't have any."

"What you mean, don't have any? Christ, does a woman gotta do everything around here?"

"They were in my other pants."

"'Course they were." Toni slapped the steering wheel. "Well. Where we sleeping tonight?"

"We need to get my brother to a hospital! That's where we're headed. Now." Alison gritted her teeth.

"Calm down, princess," said Toni. "I don't know what you're expecting, but ain't no doctors there no more."

"No one is sleeping until he gets help," Sal chimed in. "If he keeps bleeding, he'll die."

Alison sighed and held pressure on the shirts over Xander's arm. Blood drenched them. Sal put his hand over Alison's, helping her with Xander.

"I need another shirt," she said. "This one is done."

"Just stop up here at St. Henry's," said Jade. "We'll do a quick in and out. Grab some bandages…Pain meds…We'll need that shit anyway before it's picked over.

Callum's eyes lit up, and he leaned over to Toni.

"Baby, we can get some more pills. C'mon."

"Ah, hell. We don't have nowhere to go anyway."

Sal looked from Toni to Alison, to Xander. His heart sank, and tears formed like dew in his eyes. He didn't mean for his thoughts to escape his mouth when he said, "We're all going to die, aren't we?"

Alison sounded very adult in that moment. "No. No, we're not, Sal. Things aren't ever going to be the same. But we have to get through this together. That's the only option."

Xander wearily came back to consciousness.

"You sound like Mom," he said.

In the rearview mirror, the flame-engulfed zombies flickered out like candles on a birthday cake. Alison closed her eyes and made a wish—that she could be brave like Mom.

"Remember 2020, when everyone said that was the new normal?" Mo asked. "Everyone thought we would wear masks forever. The world was ending. But it didn't then. Maybe this is just another Covid."

"Shut the fuck up," said Callum. "Covid wasn't ever fucking real."

Jade snickered. "You probably think the vaccine caused all this too, huh?"

"Wouldn't be fucking surprised," replied Callum. "Not one bit."

"Don't try to talk," Alison whispered. "We're going to get you help."

CHAPTER 12

Death and decay filled the air and raped Evelyn's nostrils. An orchestra of carrion made her insides tingle. She had once walked these halls as a nurse, saving lives and comforting the ill. Now, she roamed them as a predator, hunting for the sustenance she needed to survive. The irony was not lost on her.

Was that what she was doing? Something primal had led her here, but it wasn't hunger. She was sure of it. But the scent of fresh flesh made her grow wild. She had just eaten, but her stomach panged. Her head started to become light and dizzy.

Evelyn pushed open the broken glass door and entered the hospital lobby. Fred hung back behind, careful to take in Evelyn's reaction. The once-pristine white tiles were now stained with blood and grime. The reception desk had been overturned, files and papers scattered everywhere.

She paused for a moment, memories flooding back. Evelyn remembered Janet's face, the gossiping nurses, the endless shifts.

A loud crash from deeper within the hospital snapped her out of her reverie.

Fred growled lowly. Evelyn motioned for him to follow her, and they moved silently through the wrecked corridors. The flickering fluorescent lights cast eerie shadows on the walls.

A roar echoed through the hospital.

A symphony of undead were close by, hunting. This territory had already been marked. But that didn't stop Evelyn from trekking forward. She and Fred turned a corner and found a cluster of zombies piled on top of each other, stepping on and pushing the rest aside to get through big blue doors.

The excess banged on the cafeteria windows, their tongues and mouths pressed up against the glass. Evelyn could smell what they were after before she could see them.

At least five. Two were injured.

Inside the cafeteria were familiar faces. Janet, the gossipy nurse, was there, along with a few other colleagues and patients. They were bruised, bloodied, and terrified. When Janet's eyes met Evelyn's, she gasped. Nurses held each other and patients in a cluster along the back wall.

At first, Janet was scared for Evelyn. She mouthed, *Go,* urgently pointing at the zombies poised to break down those walls any minute.

But then she got a closer look.

Fred rolled up behind Evelyn, pieces of him ripped from the bone and his head hanging limp over his shoulder.

Janet saw through Evelyn's dead eyes and the decay settling on her reanimated corpse. Evelyn's flesh was discolored, and blisters had formed on her skin. But she still looked much better than most of the undead. She was almost passing as human.

If it hadn't been for Fred's mangled state, the way he carried himself was similar. He could have passed as human too.

Fred and Evelyn approached the zombies. Evelyn's curiosity made her want a closer inspection of them. She reached out with caution and stroked the back of her hand on an undead's cheek. It was a patient. He wore the typical paper-thin hospital gown, with his ass cheeks clapping out the back.

Like a rabid animal, the patient spun around, going to swipe at Evelyn, but stopped himself. Instead, he grunted and lost track of what he had been doing. He stared deeply into Evelyn's eyes.

Leave.

Like she was an alpha controlling her pack, the patient backed down. It shuffled away from the cafeteria doors to roam the empty hallways.

Gears started to turn in Evelyn's brain. The incident with Fred wasn't stand-alone. She was different, and the others sensed it. But she couldn't fathom whether they were afraid of her or if she could control them. Evelyn had pushed her thoughts into the patient to leave. Just the one word, over and over again.

Or maybe it was coincidence.

She decided to test the waters.

Evelyn absorbed the energy around her. The static and the noise. All the ailments in her head, the tumor, the hunger, the pain—she turned it into raw energy. With all this rage, she let out a blood-curdling shriek. It reverberated throughout the hospital, like some sort of echolocation.

The few zombies digging their way toward the cafeteria stopped to admire Evelyn. Their pupils dilated, consuming the whites of their eyes completely. When they looked at her, it calmed them, and it sounded as though the ones that couldn't see her had gone into a frenzy in search of her.

After a long while, Evelyn's screech halted. Undead dispersed like low tide, making way for her.

She approached the cafeteria and put her hand on the door handle. Evelyn looked into Janet's eyes and gently tugged. The door was locked, but Evelyn didn't stop. An undead crowd watched and hissed while Evelyn twitched.

She still had a hard time speaking, but she was able to mouth to Janet, *Open the door.*

CHAPTER 13

Janet and her crew led the way, like prisoners. Evelyn kept a short distance behind.

"Please, let us go," one of the patients cried. She was an elderly woman who could barely walk. Her gait was no better than one of the undead's. "Please, I have a family."

Evelyn's lips curved into a smile.

Family. That's what I'm doing this for, she thought.

Some of the undead followed behind Evelyn. Every now and again, Evelyn would turn around and hiss at them. She didn't want to be followed. Her point had been proven, and now they were nothing more than an annoyance. Except Fred. He was useful.

When Evelyn growled, Fred started herding away more of the undead. But their fascination kept drawing them back to her.

Around Evelyn, the undead left Janet and her crew alone.

The feeble woman collapsed against the railing in the hall.

"I can't do this anymore." The old woman cried ugly tears. Her jowls shook within her palms. "Just make it quick."

The old woman had started a trend. The other few began to beg and plead with Evelyn. They coddled the old woman, asking things like, "How can you be so cruel?" and "I don't want to die."

Evelyn was tired of hearing these things. She couldn't communicate with them effectively, so she growled and roared. The others backed away from the old woman.

But the old woman still sat there. She raised a shaky hand above her face, like a shield.

Evelyn's head pulsed. That feeling was coming back. Those urges. Seeing that helpless old woman sparked something deep within her. Again, she was hungry.

Spit moistened her lips. Pockets of drool fell from her mouth. Evelyn grabbed the old woman by the neck with one hand. With ease, she pressed the old woman to the wall and brought her back to her feet. Evelyn sniffed.

The old woman smelled sickly…and suddenly less appetizing.

Arthritis and heart disease riddled the woman's body. Urine dripped down her pants legs and onto Evelyn's feet. She was terrified. Evelyn wanted to sympathize with her but couldn't. Her brain just told her she was hungry and this food was no good.

So, Evelyn let her go.

This scared the old woman enough to not speak again, to keep on her feet the best she could.

Evelyn's head pulsed again in pain. She held her face and crouched, squealing in agony. The food seemed to help this. And the longer she went without, the more her head throbbed.

"Evelyn," Janet said. "If you're still in there, I can help you."

Evelyn gazed up at her through the pain, wanting to bite Janet's head off. She charged through the crowd and grabbed Janet, tossing her to the ground.

"Wait!" Janet pleaded. Her cheeks were red with rosacea. Her eyes shook in their sockets. With a dry mouth, she licked her lips.

Desperate, she tried to console Evelyn, her former coworker.

"My keycard," she said. "Take it. Get some medicine for your head. That's what you want, right?"

Memories snapped Evelyn like a rubber band. She thought of Vera, the trial medication, how she would inject it into her forearm in secret. The faucet in the master bathroom would be running while Aaron beckoned her to bed. This was a nightly ritual. It had been the one thing that made her feel less weak. Unlike chemo and radiation, this medicine gave her a surge of power.

Evelyn hated to admit it, but Janet could have been right. Maybe she didn't have to eat people. Maybe the pain would subside with more Vera.

So, Evelyn ripped the ID card off Janet, who winced and squeezed her eyes shut, expecting Evelyn to attack. But she didn't. Instead, Evelyn breathed a low growl on Janet's face. Janet crawled away from Evelyn and wriggled by the wall, shaking.

Evelyn made an otherworldly sound at Fred. It made him more alert, sticking close.

The humans dispersed, but without the protection from Evelyn, they were quickly picked off.

The old woman went first. Those undead weren't picky eaters like Evelyn was. They chowed down, dug through her flesh. One of them tore out her heart and bit into it like a savory burger.

Meanwhile, Evelyn scanned Janet's badge to the med room. This was located on the third floor so nurses could easily access medications for their patients when needed, without being bothered to go downstairs to the first-floor pharmacy. Evelyn knew exactly where to pluck the drug. It was in a plain white box with lime-green lettering.

Vera.

Evelyn's hand trembled when she grasped the box. Memories of her life flooded back with an intensity. She noticed her reflection in the shiny metal of a medical cabinet—a stark reminder of the person she used to be. Her eyes, once full of life, now only reflected hunger and pain. It scared her, how empty she had looked.

Fred stood guard at the door, his eyes scanning the hallway for any threats. He was fiercely loyal to Evelyn, and his presence gave her a strange sense of comfort.

She tore open the box, pulling out a vial of Vera along with a syringe. Her hands, now unsteady, struggled to draw the medication into the needle.

Cool liquid surged through Evelyn's veins when she injected the drug. A burst of euphoria coursed through her. Immediately, the pounding in her head began to subside.

Fred started making noises, signaling Evelyn.

"Evelyn…" Janet's voice was shaky, but it held a glimmer of hope. She had followed Evelyn to the med room, keeping a safe distance. "Are you okay? Do you remember me?"

Evelyn growled in Janet's direction.

CHAPTER 14

Toni pulled up to the emergency room at St. Henry's Hospital.

"This is a bad idea."

"You don't have to come," replied Alison.

"Don't go," Xander whispered. He was fading in and out of consciousness. But at least he hadn't turned into one of them.

"I'll go," offered Mo. "Me and Sal, right?"

Sal looked over at Mo in surprise. "Why do you care?"

"You saved me. I'm returning the favor. This is your friend. So, we'd be even."

"Deal," said Sal. "Me and Mo will be quick, in and out. The pharmacy is on the first floor. Should be quick. Alison, you stay with Xander.

"Sal, no. I'm going in there."

"I'll go," replied Xander. "Let me figure out my own shit."

"We all go," said Jade. "Any plan other than that is suicide."

The group crept in, glass shards crunching beneath their feet. A few zombies yowled, caught in the wreckage of fallen building pieces and car crashes, just out of reach of them.

Mo got close to the top half of one of the zombies. He didn't know him. None of the group did. The zombie's teeth chattered, inches away from Mo, while he examined.

"They look sad," he said.

Medical carts and gurneys with patients still strapped to them had been toppled over. Some groaned for help, but mangled zombies that were missing limbs didn't pose much threat.

Footsteps rumbled in the nearby stairwell. A small group of people hurried down the stairs at full speed. Behind them was a herd of the undead. The zombies stopped when they caught a slow person, sharing the feast amongst each other.

A thicker woman in nursing attire pushed past Alison, who helped Sal hold Xander up. Her baby blue scrubs were coated in blood. She ran so fast, her tears flew from her face.

But something made her stop.

She looked at the group, sheer terror in her eyes.

"You…You're Evelyn's kids, aren't you?"

Riddled with gibberish in between, Janet did her best to explain to them about Evelyn upstairs. How something was off with her.

"Mom…" Alison's brows furrowed.

"I don't want to say it, but…I told you so," said Sal.

Xander was nodding off again. His body slumped, and the dead weight caused Alison's knees to buckle. Sal could barely hold Xander himself.

"Woah, woah woah," said Sal.

Xander's eyes moved rapidly, and consciousness slipped through.

"We have to save her…" he said. "She's not like them."

"You gotta get out of here," replied the nurse. "If this didn't kill her, the cancer will."

"We don't have time for this shit," said Jade. "Callum, come with me to the pharmacy."

The group—minus Sal, Xander, and Alison—moved on to the pharmacy. Alison stood silently, lips quivering.

"Allie…" Sal slumped Xander against the wall and went to her aid, but she didn't respond.

With free hands, he reached for the bow slung over his back. He aimed at the two undead in the stairwell, who were finishing their meal. One arrow split and bounced against the wall, but Sal quickly recovered and domed them both.

"'Course that bitch didn't tell you." The nurse rolled her eyes. "Fuck around and find out. I'm out."

The nurse left.

Not long after, her screams echoed outside, along with the shuffling noises of undead nearing the hospital. Alison's breath quickened when she heard Janet's cries, and reality sunk in.

Sal reloaded his bow.

"Be smart about this," he said. "While Xander is still somewhat conscious, you carry him behind the pharmacy counter, and I'll guard you. We can't both be unarmed and walking bait."

Alison heard Sal but couldn't respond. She rested her hand on the gun tucked within her waistband, but Sal placed his hand on hers.

"You won't need that. I'll protect you."

Jade and Callum were ahead with weapons raised, covering each other's backs. Toni followed close behind. Mo ran with the bags, rushing to keep up.

Callum smashed an undead's head with the stock of his rifle. Jade finished it off with the Sawzall, the vibrating blades slicing through the zombie's brain. It hummed and made a clatter.

"Sorry," Jade whispered, kicking the zombie in the chest to free her weapon. Then she turned it off.

Groans of more undead lingered in the near distance.

"Quiet, dumbass." Toni snatched the empty bag Mo was holding and hopped the counter. She started to scan the shelves of medication, whispering the names of them to herself quickly. "Bingo."

She had located the narcotics and was swiping an armful into the satchel.

"Found bandages," announced Jade.

"Antiseptic here," said Mo.

Alison hovered in the doorway, a frantic mess, propping Xander against the counter.

"Have some Vicodin." Toni tossed an orange bottle to Alison.

Sal trailed in shortly after, preparing another arrow as he backed through the entryway. Jade and Mo rushed over to help bandage Xander's wound and keep it from getting infected.

"He's so pale, he's gray. He's lost too much blood already," Jade said.

Shambling footsteps, groans, and growls festered, growing closer to the group.

Alison poked a pill through Xander's lips, but he was too far gone to swallow.

"What's your mum's name? Evelyn?" Callum held up a plastic bag with her name on it, which contained a plethora of medications. "She's a goddamn junkie."

He laughed, tossing the bag to Sal.

Sal peered into the bag, noticing small bottles with a green, translucent liquid and syringes. He picked up one of the bottles to inspect it.

"Christ…" he said.

Alison couldn't focus between her brother's fading light and everything else around her.

"What's that?" she asked.

"Just says…Vera. Nothing else. Guess it was probably for the, uh…you know."

Alison nodded. She rubbed Xander's forehead, where beads of sweat had gathered.

"Cancer." Alison finished Sal's sentence, despite him trying to be delicate.

He dropped the bag to the ground and the vial.

"She was already dead," said Alison.

"Hey. No, she wasn't." Sal went to comfort her.

She was more receptive this time, falling into his arms.

"But now she is." Jade gave Sal a look like he better shut up.

"We're trapped!" Mo called.

Everyone looked up to see what Mo was talking about.

A horde was cautiously approaching, closing in on them. And in the center was their leader, Evelyn.

Everyone readied their weapons—everyone except Alison.

"I knew we should have let that kid die," mumbled Toni.

"Your gun, kid." Callum elbowed Alison.

But Evelyn put up her hand and halted. The undead stopped in their tracks and didn't move any closer.

Alison's voice broke. "…Mom."

Xander, now slightly more coherent from the hastily administered painkillers, glanced up, saw his mother, then turned to his sister.

"Don't, Allie," he whispered.

His legs shook when he shoved Alison aside and tried to stand.

"Not her." He heaved, struggling to breathe.

Xander went to use his hand to steady himself, and his eyes widened. The shock of losing his extremity hadn't settled in. He flexed his bloodied arm and grasped where his hand should have been.

"No sudden movements." Mo shifted over the counter with caution and got in his martial arts stance.

Callum didn't remove his eye from the scope. He had it aimed at Evelyn's head.

She turned to him and smiled.

"Mom, I know you're still in there," Alison said, tears streaming down her face. "We need you. Xander needs you."

Evelyn approached slowly, dragging her feet across the floor. One zombie limped behind, drooling. The rest of the horde stood open-jawed, with nothing behind their eyes. Waiting.

Evelyn's hand twitched, and she let out a low, guttural growl. She looked at Alison, then to Xander, and for a moment, she bore some semblance of her old self. Evelyn lurched forward, arm extended to her children.

Alison crawled over the counter on her hands and knees. Sal grabbed her by the ankle, but she kicked him off.

"That's it. We're out of here," said Toni. "C'mon, Callum."

She nudged his shoulder, but his eyes were locked on his target.

Much like Evelyn, the building itself groaned. The ceiling wailed, and the structure shook. Fragments of dust fell from overhead, and a small crack emerged in the ceiling panel.

Alison noticed it.

She leaped over the counter and, at full track-star speed, lunged in front of Evelyn, knocking her back before a piece of the building collapsed.

Evelyn saw her coming. She put her hands up and hissed, desperate to stop her daughter. Both missed the fallen wreckage by a thin margin.

Also in that moment, there was a gunshot.

***

Smoke rose from the barrel of the rifle and weaved in with the dust from the wreckage.

Callum had missed his target and hit Alison instead. Her lifeless body pooled blood on the floor. Debris fell onto her and smashed into her back. Then her head popped like a water balloon.

A large cluster of zombies funneled through the hole in the ceiling. Evelyn trembled over her daughter's body. Crumpled pieces of drywall and beams caved in around her. But she was in another place. She looked Callum dead in the eyes and screamed.

The zombies entering through the ceiling and the ones in Evelyn's trance broke their calm states and went feral.

Callum unloaded his gun, picking off as many as he could. Jade screamed and sprayed guts with her Sawzall. Bodies piled on top of each other, like a barricade over the pharmacy counter. Even Sal joined in, until he fingered his last arrow. He put it back in the quiver and sighed, looking out at the horde.

But Xander just watched his screaming mother.

With immense speed, she lunged at him. Bullets trailed behind her, merely grazing her rotten flesh. One clipped her cheek, which silenced her scream. In a whirlwind, she gutted Callum, snatched up Xander, and fled, letting the undead army consume the rest of them.

Mo's intestines were ripped from his gut. A group of three slurped up his bowels like spaghetti.

Toni's knuckles were raw from using her fist weapon, and she was out of breath. She missed and landed a hit on one's mouth. But the undead unhinged its jaw and snapped down on her wrist. She was overwhelmed by a blanket of zombies.

Jade's blade caught in the side of an undead. The motor on the Sawzall had died, and she couldn't pull her weapon free. A crawling zombie latched onto her leg, and she fell to the floor in front of Alison. Blood gurgled from her mouth onto Alison's face.

Sal was bitten, but he managed to escape through a vent above the shelves of medication. He army crawled through the metal hallway, his calf burning in pain. Sal dragged himself through the narrow tunnel, the metallic taste of blood filling his mouth. His injured calf throbbed in agony.

***

Evelyn darted past the mess of death and undead, a wave of zombies parting out of her way. She clutched Xander tightly to her chest, her growls punctuated by Xander's weak, labored breaths. Evelyn stopped in a small, abandoned operating room, cradling her son gently on a gurney.

Xander shook and shoved his mother off him with his injured arm. He feebly crawled to the outermost edge of the room.

Evelyn positioned a heavy table in front of the door to block visitors. She reached around and grabbed up the vials she had stolen from the med room. Her arms and legs tingled, and she struggled to command her body's movement. Finally, she stabbed the needle into the green liquid, and it slurped into the syringe.

"Mom…Are you in there?"

Evelyn groaned and inspected the needle. She tapped it lightly, like a cat batting around a toy on a string. Evelyn's head throbbed. Her world shook within her vision. The static of Xander calling, "Mom," echoed through her ears. Her vision blurred like the white noise of an old television. Even the greens and magenta she could actually see faded into gray. Her stomach growled.

Xander got closer, and Evelyn leveraged the syringe between them.

All she had to do was stab her thigh and inject the medicine.

It would subside.

The hunger.

But it.

He.

Xander grabbed his mother by the wrist with his good hand and stopped her. They locked eyes.

"Please," Xander whispered. "Come back to us."

The burning in Evelyn's head surged throughout her entire body. The temptation of such tender flesh was too much. Her urges won.

Evelyn dropped the syringe and unhinged her jaw. She let out one final scream before throwing Xander to the ground.

With only one hand, Xander was no match. He grabbed her throat, but she was too strong. Drool slid from her mouth and into his.

"I love you, Mom," he cried.

Evelyn's rancid breath fumed into Xander's face. He cried and closed his eyes.

But instead of being bitten and eaten by his mother, her body collapsed onto his.

Evelyn's head slumped, with an arrow from one ear through the other.

***

Xander started hyperventilating, yelling unintelligible things. Sal hopped down from a vent and consoled his friend. He peeled Evelyn's body off him, but Xander didn't get up. Instead, he threw his feet and fists in a flurry of blows at Sal, like a child throwing a tantrum.

Sal took the bow off his shoulder, along with the emptied quiver, and tried to calm Xander.

"*Shhh, shh*. They'll hear us, man. Please, please, please, *shhh*."

Adrenaline pumped through Xander. He pushed himself up and knocked over a tray of operating tools. Xander clenched a pair of forceps and, before Sal could even react, repeatedly stabbed his best friend in the face.

Memories of their childhood flooded through his head, but Xander screamed and continued to attack his friend.

Memories of freeze pops after the only win their Little League team ever achieved.

Memories of GBA link cables and drawling through the dungeons of *Doom*.

Memories of him trading a date with his sister for tickets to an R-rated movie because Sal's mom had been cool about that stuff, but Alison had been pissed.

Memories of their Ghostface costumes, plastic knives with fake blood inside of them that dripped from side to side.

This thought made Xander's heart hurt.

He dropped the forceps and sat back on his bottom.

Sal's blood covered him completely. There was so much, he was drowning in it, barely able to breathe through the sea of red.

Suddenly, Xander felt outside of his consciousness, like a spectator watching the events. He thought of the people who had died trying to help him. Xander thought of Alison and then his mother. He crawled over to Evelyn.

"It's okay, Mom. Just like before."

A shine caught his attention—the green liquid in a syringe close to Evelyn's corpse.

"This is it, isn't it? What kept you alive?"

Xander grabbed the syringe and jabbed it into his mother's arm, injecting the fluids. He shook her and waited.

"Wake up, Mom. Come on…Come on."

Another vial of green liquid rolled away from him while he rummaged around the floor, feeling for something that would help. His fingers trembled, grabbing the bottle. He wedged it between his side and his bad arm and picked up the syringe again.

Like his mother had done, Xander stabbed the needle through the top of the bottle. The shock of his hand missing hit him again when the pain returned, searing through his veins. He dropped the vial and syringe.

Agony crawled through his body. His organs started to shut down, and he collapsed to the ground beside his mother, going from convulsions to completely still. Her dead eyes soon matched his.

And then his head throbbed.

It throbbed with a pain unlike any he had known before.

About the Author

You can find Jenny in the underbrush of the woods listening to the secrets the wind shares with the rustling leaves. In the shadows of nature, she finds her inspiration for dark poetry, metaphysical nonfiction, and horror.

She resides in the suburbia of Michigan with her daughter Luna. When she's not writing, she's reading, casting spells, playing video games, and getting her soul sucked out by corporate America. She has been writing since first grade when she wrote a book called The Roaring Tiger for her classmates. The awe of those kids getting whisked away into her story cultivated a love for the craft ever since.

Jenny has four other titles published and available from Amazon and other platforms. In January 2026, she will have her debut horror novel with WTHP, called: *The Blurry Man.*

Acknowledgements

Lyndsey Smith – Owner of Horrorsmith Editing – Lyndsey is an awesome editor to work with, and I will recommend her services to everyone I know.

Ruth Anna Evans – Author of Against Medical Advice – Not only is Ruth a talented author, she also makes amazing covers. Thanks, Ruth, for helping me bring my visions to life.

Luna – My daughter – I love you, Luna, to the moon and back. I dedicate this book to you and all future books I will put out there. You can accomplish anything you put in the effort for. Whether it be art, writing, video editing – you name it. You don't have to choose one thing. I'm proud of you.

www.ingramcontent.com/pod-product-compliance
Lightning Source LLC
Chambersburg PA
CBHW071155300726
48975CB00004B/1161